I0553360

DESERT MANNA BOOK 2

JOY FOR MOURNING

Karen Baney

desert life
media

Joy for Mourning: Desert Manna Book 2
By Karen Baney

Copyright © 2022 by Karen Baney
Cover Design by Karen Baney

Unless otherwise indicated, all Scripture quotations are from The ESV® Bible (The Holy Bible, English Standard Version®), copyright © 2001 by Crossway, a publishing ministry of Good News Publishers. Used by permission. All rights reserved.

All scripture quotations marked as NIV are taken from the Holy Bible, New International Version®, NIV®. Copyright ©1973, 1978, 1984 by Biblica, Inc.™ Used by permission of Zondervan. All rights reserved worldwide. www.zondervan.com

All rights reserved. No part of this publication may be reproduced, distributed, or transmitted in any form or by any means, including photocopying, recording, or other electronic or mechanical methods, without the prior written permission of the publisher, except in the case of brief quotations embodied in critical reviews and certain other noncommercial uses permitted by copyright law. For permission requests, write to the publisher at the address below.

Publisher:
Desert Life Media, LLC
Gilbert, AZ 85295

www.karenbaney.com

Printed in the United States of America

ISBN-979-8-9858202-3-2

This is a work of fiction. Names, characters, businesses, places, events, and incidents are either the products of the author's imagination or used in a fictitious manner. Any resemblance to actual persons, living or dead, or actual events is purely coincidental.

The Spirit of the Sovereign Lord is on me,
because the Lord has anointed me
to proclaim good news to the poor.
He has sent me to bind up the brokenhearted,
to proclaim freedom for the captives
and release from darkness for the prisoners,
to proclaim the year of the Lord's favor
and the day of vengeance of our God,
to comfort all who mourn,
and provide for those who grieve in Zion—
to bestow on them
a crown of beauty instead of ashes,
the oil of joy instead of mourning,
and a garment of praise
instead of a spirit of despair.
They will be called oaks of righteousness,
a planting of the Lord
for the display of his splendor.
—Isaiah 61:1-3 NIV

CHAPTER I

Fort Goodwin, Arizona Territory
May 25, 1865

Captain Joshua Harrison led his company of mounted cavalry toward the Gila River Basin away from Fort Goodwin. The sun beat down on his back which caused sweat to trickle between his shoulder blades. Sergeant Dixon Pike rode up next to him on his chestnut gelding as they neared Widow Feagan's property.

"No smoke coming from her chimney today," Joshua said.

"Cap, want me to ride over?" the sergeant asked.

"I'll come with you."

As the pair rode away from the rest of the men, loud screams pierced the air behind them. Joshua pulled back on the reins and turned his palomino gelding toward the noise. A group of thirty Apache swarmed the rest of his unit.

Without waiting for an order, the sergeant headed toward the melee as Joshua followed closely behind. He drew his sword and speared the first Apache he saw. The man slid from the end of his sword falling to the ground. Another Apache warrior's high-pitched screams came from his left. Sergeant Pike shot him with his revolver. Soon a swarm of Apache surrounded them.

The young corporal assigned to his company last week was pulled from his horse. The warriors slit his throat and stripped him of his hair. Joshua clenched his jaw. Another corporal caught a tomahawk with his chest and fell backwards off his horse. The moment his body landed on the ground the Apache braves overtook him.

"Fall back!" Joshua issued the order, but only he and Sergeant Pike remained.

"Cap!" the sergeant warned him.

Joshua turned. A young Apache warrior launched himself toward Joshua and pulled him from his horse. He landed hard on the ground. His breath left in a rush.

The warrior connected a blow to Joshua's stomach. Then he punched him in the face. Joshua raised his arms as the warrior brought down his fist again. Another man joined the warrior. He kicked Joshua in the stomach repeatedly. He moaned and rolled onto his side. He curled up while blows continued to connect with his body. Then something forceful hit his head and his vision blurred. Then it faded to blackness.

When Joshua woke sometime later, he laid on the ground in front of a fire. His hands and feet were bound. An older Apache man noticed his movement. The man pulled out a long knife and sliced Joshua's shirt off his body. Then he took the knife and ran it down one leg of Joshua's pants and then the other. He ripped the clothing from his body.

Another brave joined him. He held Joshua's head back and said something he did not understand. Then he took a knife and twisted the point into his chest slowly, turning the blade round and round. Joshua bit the inside of his cheek to keep from screaming. The Indian removed the blade leaving a hole two inches in diameter, but only a quarter inch deep. Blood oozed from the wound down his bare abdomen.

The older man stuck his finger in the wound. Joshua writhed in pain until he passed out.

Sometime later, Joshua woke. The smell of blood and dirt overwhelmed him. He shivered as bugs crawled across his skin in the blackness. He could not see. His hands and feet were no longer bound. He felt around the small space. Cold dirt and silt. As he stretched out his arm to find the boundaries of his prison, pain tore through his side. Bile spewed from his mouth.

He fell backwards and his spine pressed up against the damp dirt wall. He looked up. A small circle of light appeared overhead. He had to be at least thirty or forty feet below the opening of the pit.

He crawled along the dirt floor. His hand connected with something sharp. It pierced his skin. He lifted his hand but could not see the warm blood as it trickled down his arm. He tried to move forward, but there were more sharp pointy things on the ground in front of him.

Joshua sat down with his back against the dirt wall. He drew his long legs up to his chest and rested his head on his knees. *Lord, help.*

A rodent squeaked and scurried nearby. Its long tail flicked Joshua's foot. He sucked in a sharp breath and pain seared through his middle. Exhaustion washed over him and pulled him under.

Day after day he sat in that dark, dank pit. No one came for him. No one provided food or water. He shivered then burned. Sweat rolled down his naked back which caused more dirt to stick to his skin. Each breath caused a sharp pain in his side.

The longer he went without food or water, the worse he felt. He had no energy to find an escape. He would die in the pit soon. He thought he was ready and prayed he would not suffer much longer.

CHAPTER 2

Prescott, Arizona Territory
August 7, 1872

Sometimes life was not fair. Things did not go as planned.

When Grace Talbert first accepted Alex Glassman's offer of courtship, she hoped it would lead to a relationship full of romance, love, and eventually marriage. He would make the perfect husband. He was handsome and intelligent. He was a godly man. They were good friends.

Unfortunately, after eight months, Alex still had not proposed. In a way, she supposed she was relieved, especially since the spark she hoped would materialize never did. She wished she could conjure something more. He was a good man and so much better than most of the potential suitors Daddy foisted on her over the years.

No, the problem was that she just did not love him in the way a woman should love her future husband. She was certain he did not love her either.

There was only one solution: she needed to break off her courtship and set them both free.

She sighed as she headed downstairs. She let Kingsley, her butler, know that she would be gone for an hour, then she stepped outside.

The sun warmed her arms, and she adjusted her parasol to shade them. She wore a pale pink dress with a bustle. Folds of fabric on the skirt were edged with black lace. She chose the dress because even though it flattered her, it gave her a calmer and kind appearance. Delivering the news to Alex would be difficult and she desired they part on good terms.

As she neared Alex's office, she squared her shoulders and lifted her chin. She opened the door and walked in. The walls were painted a deep burgundy with dark walnut wainscoting. Glided sconces holding oil lamps flanked the sides of cheerful artwork lined with large ornate golden frames. The decor of the office spoke of Alex's success.

She smiled as she entered the building.

"Morning, Miss Talbert," Bradley Whitaker, Alex's secretary, greeted her. "His meeting should be finished shortly. Feel free to have a seat."

Grace declined and stood in front of the painting on the wall in the lobby. She pretended to study the landscape, while her mind churned. She knew she had to be the one to break it off. Daddy always seemed to go easier on her than on the prospective suitor when her relationships ended. The last thing Alex needed while campaigning for District Attorney was to make an enemy of the powerful Simon Talbert.

Alex held open the door to his office as his client left. When he saw her waiting in the lobby, he frowned. "Did I forget we had plans?"

Grace straightened her back and entered his office. Alex followed and closed his door. He walked to her and gave her a peck on the cheek.

She sat down in the guest chair as Alex rounded his dark walnut desk and sat on the other side.

"What brings you here?" he asked. His face remained impassive. She supposed it served him well in the courtroom, but poorly in a courtship.

"Alex, I need to break off our courtship."

He stood to his feet and leaned forward, placing both hands flat on the top of his desk. "Why?"

She frowned at him. He sighed and sat down again.

"I know my ideals and charitable works with the Indians hurt your political ambitions even though you have Daddy's support."

"Grace," his voice softened. "I am not courting you for my political gain." His forehead creased. "Yes, your desire to help every cause of the downtrodden, especially the Indians, is problematic. But we can overcome that."

"How? I'm planning a trip next week to deliver the food and clothing the Women's Aid Society has collected. I'll be headed down to Camp Date Creek. How do you propose to overcome that?"

"You could step down as President of the organization."

"Never." She straightened her back and narrowed her eyes. He was asking her to give up the one thing that gave her life purpose and meaning.

Alex let out a long, slow breath. "Then we are at an impasse."

She snorted. "That is my point. You knew about my ideals before courting me. Yet you want me to give up the things I am most passionate about."

"When we marry, you will not need to work. I will provide for you. If this relationship is to succeed, then we need to come to some compromise."

"One where you get what you want, and I become some docile domestic? Besides, I do not need to work now. I do not get paid for running the Women's Aid Society. I run it because I want to help those less fortunate, including the Indians."

Alex shook his head. "You are being unreasonable."

She raised her chin. "We are not a good match. I do not love you. You do not love me. Though we are friends, I am looking for something more."

He propped his elbows on the desk and steepled his fingers but said nothing further.

"I know dealing with Daddy can be difficult, so I will be the one to break this off. He will chastise me and then forgive me all in the same breath. That way you can save face with him, and your political future will be intact."

"Grace—"

"We both know this relationship will never go beyond friendship."

A knock sounded at the door. Bradley opened it a crack. "Miss Talbert there's a—"

"Miss Talbert," Kingsley said out of breath. "It's your mother. Come quickly."

Grace shot to her feet and followed Kingsley out the door. She paused speaking over her shoulder. "It's over Alex. I have nothing more to say."

Kingsley hurried her down the street at a fast walk. She wanted to hike up her skirts and run the rest of the way home for Kingsley would not have come if Mama was not in dire need of her.

He held the front door open, and Grace ran upstairs to Mama's room.

"Mama, I'm here."

Daddy sat on the edge of the bed stroking Mama's stringy silver hair. Her skin was gray and thin. Dark circles made her eyes look sunken deep in her head. She looked so frail, worse than she had this morning before Grace left.

Her eyes fluttered open. Her voice was weak when she said Grace's name.

Grace rushed to her side and took her hand as she sat on the edge of her bed. She stroked it murmuring soothing sounds as she had done countless times before.

"Marry for love, my dear one. No matter what."

The words hit Grace's heart to the core. It was what she desired despite Daddy's many attempts to see her paired with someone for his own benefit. She and Mama often spoke of the importance of a love match.

"Mama!" Her voice cracked. Tears streamed down her face as she realized her mama's life was ending.

Mama coughed so hard the bed shook. Blood dribbled down her chin and Daddy wiped it away with his handkerchief.

"I. Love. You. Both." The words were a whisper.

Then the air left Mama's lungs and her hand grew cold as her body went limp. Daddy cried out as if someone had reached into his chest and physically ripped his heart from his body. Her heart broke watching his raw grief.

Grace lifted Mama's hand to her lips and kissed it.

"Goodbye, Mama," she whispered. "No more tears and no more pain for you now."

Daddy was inconsolable. Grace tried to get him to leave Mama's side, but he leaned over and kissed her face and stroked her hair. For all of Simon Talbert's faults, he did love his wife and daughter with all his heart.

Grace left the room and closed the door behind her. She would check on him soon. Then she headed downstairs to tell the staff.

"Kingsley," she said, squaring her shoulders, "Gather the staff."

Within a few minutes, Kingsley brought Mercy and Esther into the parlor. "Mrs. Talbert passed away a few moments ago. She is finally at peace."

The maid and cook cried and hugged each other. Kingsley sniffed and looked down at the floor. All three of them had come over with the family from London when Grace was a little girl. They, too, had watched Mama's steady decline and losing battle with consumption.

"Please see that a tray is brought up to my room for supper. Have something ready for Daddy, should he call for you, though I doubt he will today. And, Kingsley," she said turning her attention to him, "please have Daddy's secretary meet me in his office in an hour to discuss final arrangements."

Kingsley replied, "Yes, Miss Grace."

Grace climbed the stairs and hid in the solace of her bedroom. After closing the door behind her, she leaned against it and slid down to the floor. She hugged her legs and wept.

CHAPTER 3

A knock sounded on Grace's door. She was not sure how long she cried, leaning against it.

Kingsley said, "Theodore is waiting in Mr. Talbert's office."

She cleared her throat. "I'll be right there."

Grace stood and poured some water into the wash basin, then splashed it on her face. She patted it dry with a towel. She checked her appearance in the mirror and decided it was good enough for the task at hand.

She peeked into her mama's room. Daddy still clung to Mama whispering words of love to his dead wife.

"Daddy, you must come," she said gently as she touched his shoulder. He moved back like a limp doll in her hands. Then he finally stood. She led him to his bedroom.

"Why don't you rest in here for a while."

Daddy kissed her cheek and laid down in his bed. She pulled his shoes off and then kissed his forehead. Then she left and closed the door behind her.

Her stomach growled, but she ignored it. Instead, she went downstairs.

"Theodore," she greeted Daddy's secretary as she entered his study.

The young man was short. He wore a dark brown suit with a vest and bow tie. His eyes were dark but full of sympathy as he took his usual seat in the navy-blue upholstered chair across from the large cherry wood desk.

She told him the news as she took a seat in Daddy's leather chair behind the desk. "We need to make arrangements. Daddy is heartbroken and will need some time, so whatever you can handle would be appreciated."

"Yes, Miss Talbert. I will head over to the undertaker straight away. Mr. and Mrs. Talbert prepared for this day, so I am aware of their wishes and will see their plan through."

"Thank you, Theodore." She was relieved that she would not have to manage the arrangements.

He took his leave.

Grace leaned back in Daddy's chair and tilted her head back. She stared at the white ceiling. Swirls added texture to the plaster ceiling. She tried to find a repeated pattern, but nothing was an exact match.

Mama was gone.

She sniffed. Mama was sick for so long. She first became ill with consumption when they lived in San Francisco over six years ago. The doctors did little to help her. Daddy scoured the newspapers and wrote letters to many physicians to find a cure or a treatment. Finally, one doctor suggested in a letter that Mama might benefit from drier air, like what could be found in the Arizona Territory. So, five years ago, Daddy uprooted them to Prescott.

Grace did not mind. She was not fond of San Francisco. It seemed too wild compared to her earlier childhood memories of London. Prescott was much smaller than both cities. But it was quaint. Homey. Full of kind people, well at least the ones she worked with at church or at the Women's Aid Society.

Daddy often said that while Prescott was good for Mama, it was not as good for Grace. He lamented on more than one occasion how difficult it would be to find a suitable husband for her. Of course, his idea of a suitable husband was far different from hers. Daddy presented Grace with business associates, often someone he felt would benefit his position in a business matter or his standing in the town. None of the suitors were horrible men. Most were kind to her and appreciated her beauty. A few even appreciated her mind and her charitable works. But not one of them had captured her heart.

Daddy's pattern remained the same. He would give Grace's heart time to heal when she broke off a relationship. Little did he know that no healing was necessary. She had not been brokenhearted over a single one. Then Daddy would find the next eligible wealthy young suitor who would benefit him. Though, the last year or so the suitors were getting older. She was twenty-two. Alex just turned thirty-one.

When Grace found fault in the passionless relationships, she and Daddy usually argued. He presented all the reasons why the suitor was a good match. She pointed out that she did not love the suitor. Mama often acted as the mediator, reminding her husband of the importance of love and how it enhanced their relationship. Daddy would acquiesce.

What would she do without Mama? A sob lodged in her throat.

"Miss Grace," Esther, the cook, said from the doorway. "I have the tray you requested. Do you still want it in your room?"

"No. I'll take it over on the settee." She stood and walked over to the settee facing the fireplace then sat down.

When Esther set the tray on the coffee table, Grace thanked her. "Can you send Mercy to light a fire?"

"Yes, Miss Grace."

Though it was early August, and the days were warm, the evenings sometimes chilled. She did not need the fire for warmth, though gazing at the flames would soothe her hurting soul.

She took the plate with several finger sandwiches and balanced it in her lap. She ate two then returned the plate to the tray, unable to eat more.

Mercy, the maid, lit the fire and Grace leaned back in the settee.

Knowing Mama's passing was coming did not make it any easier. Year after year, her grief took different forms. She grieved when Mama no longer felt well enough to go to church with her. Her heart broke when Mama was too sick to join her and Daddy for supper. When Mama began sharing wisdom about marriage and encouraged Grace not to accept Daddy's choice for her, she realized that Mama was trying to leave her with the advice she had hoped to give her daughter in the future. She knew it was unlikely that Mama would see her get married.

Tears trickled down her face and she wiped them away. A log in the fireplace popped. Little sparks floated and disappeared up the chimney. She felt numb. Mama was truly gone. No longer would she receive advice from her. No longer would she share her hopes and dreams with her.

"Miss Grace," Kingsley said from the doorway. "You have a visitor."

Grace sighed. She was in no mood for company of any kind.

"It's Mr. Glassman."

"Tell him to go away," she said as she wrapped her arms around her waist.

"Grace," Alex's voice came from behind her.

She did not stand or acknowledge him.

He came around in front of the settee blocking her view of the fire. "Is everything alright?"

"No. Mama passed a few hours ago."

He kneeled in front of her. "Oh, Grace, I'm so sorry."

When he took her hand, she pulled it away. "Please don't make this harder than it already is. I was firm in my decision to break off our courtship. While I appreciate your visit, you should go."

He touched her chin and turned her head to look at him. He searched her eyes for several seconds until she looked away. Then Alex stood slowly, offered his condolences, and left.

"Grace," Daddy said as he entered the room. "Did I hear you correctly? Have you broken off your courtship?"

She patted the seat next to her. "Esther left these sandwiches. You should eat."

Daddy sat next to her and placed his arm around her shoulders. He looked years older than he had that morning. She leaned her head against his chest.

"Did you?"

"Yes, Daddy. This morning, before…" Her voice broke.

"Why sweetheart?"

She whispered, "I don't love him."

He placed a kiss on the top of her head. "I'm sorry."

They sat there for a long time until the room grew darker after the sun set. Then she took her leave and retired to her room. The losses of the day weighed heavily on her heart.

———

Two days later, Grace donned a black dress. She wound her blond hair into a tight knot at the base of her neck.

Then she placed the matching black hat on top and secured it with a few hat pins.

When she arrived in the parlor her daddy sat in his favorite chair and stared out the window. He looked lost. She stood next to him and leaned down to place a kiss on his cheek.

"It's time, Daddy."

He nodded and stood. She led him to the carriage waiting in front of their home.

The ride to the cemetery outside of town only took a few minutes. A few of her daddy's business associates were waiting. Alex was too. He moved forward to help her out of the carriage.

"Just thought you could use a friend," he hurriedly explained.

"Thank you."

She accepted his hand and stepped down from the carriage. When she let go of his hand, she raised her chin walked toward the grave site without another word.

Daddy stood next to her and nodded for the pastor to begin.

Moisture clouded her vision. She retrieved her handkerchief and dabbed the corners of her eyes.

There were so few people there to say their goodbyes to Mama. The household staff, herself, and Daddy were the only ones who even knew Mama. The rest were there presumably to garner favor with her or, more likely, Daddy.

A wagon rode down the street and Grace looked up. Her gaze connected with the blue eyes of a total stranger. He gave her a heavy nod and his mouth curved down. His forehead creased for a moment before he looked away.

He lost someone too. She felt it across the distance.

Grace followed the wagon with her eyes until it descended the hill into town out of view.

The pastor finished speaking kind words and reading scripture over Mama. Then her coffin was lowered into the ground. Grace stepped forward to toss a handful of dirt on Mama's grave. A sob escaped Daddy's lips as he did the same. He coughed trying to mask it, but she heard it. She knew his heart ached beyond words.

She placed her hand in the crook of his arm and led him to the carriage.

Within minutes they were back in the quiet of their own home. Neither of them wanted visitors. They did not see the need since Mama had been bedridden most of their time in Prescott. She never ventured beyond their home so no one in town knew her.

As they sat in the parlor the staff hovered nearby, far enough away to give them space but close enough should they need anything.

Mama was gone. A sob choked Grace's throat. After all the years of illness and close calls, her mama finally found relief in death.

"There, there," Daddy whispered and moved to sit next to her. Tears streamed down his face.

"Aren't we quite the pair," Grace said. She sniffed and straightened.

He nodded wiping his face with his handkerchief.

Exhaustion washed over her, and she excused herself. She went to her room and laid down to suffer her grief in private until she fell asleep.

CHAPTER 4

Joshua's long journey neared its end. Coming back to Prescott was bittersweet. Bitter for it reminded him of the friend he lost. Bitter for a lost love. Yet, sweet because his company was thriving and growing. Sweet because his daughter was at his side.

He needed a change of scenery. Tucson felt crowded. Too many memories of his time in the Army. Though he had been in the Army when he lived at Fort Whipple, outside of Prescott, he had spent so little time there. It had far fewer sad memories.

The move was as much for Victoria as it was for him. Joshua had a hard time finding a good housekeeper who he trusted to take care of her when he traveled. The last housekeeper had only been employed with him for three months before he caught her with an unsavory man in his home while Victoria was upstairs in her room. He suspected from the beginning that she was stealing from him, but when he came home to that scene, he let her go.

After that incident, Joshua stayed home which was good for Victoria but difficult for his business. He was the name behind the company. He and his best friend worked hard to build the business into what it was. Joshua was the one with the contacts in the military. He needed to travel to help the business grow.

Victoria was eleven. He wanted her to feel safe walking to and from school whether he was home or on the road. He wanted her to finish school in a smaller town with wholesome people. That's how he remembered his friends from eight years ago. Wholesome good people.

As the wagon crested the last hill headed down into Prescott, Joshua noticed the small funeral at the cemetery. A young woman clung to an older man, likely her father. When the wagon lurched over a bump in the road and squeaked in protest, her gaze locked with his. Her pain and sadness mirrored his own. He nodded hoping to convey his condolences to the stranger with silky blond hair and gray-blue eyes.

"Are we almost there?" Victoria asked, breaking him away from his thoughts.

He looked over at her. She twisted one of her long dark curls around her finger. Her bright blue eyes looked tired, and he heard the hint of a whine in her voice. She looked so much like her mother it sometimes hurt to look at her.

"Almost. Just a few more minutes."

She sighed. "Good. I'm sore from sitting in this wagon."

Joshua laughed and tapped a finger lightly on her nose. Leave it to her to pull him from his pensive mood.

A lot changed in eight years. The town was four times larger than he remembered—maybe more. Wide streets were flanked with houses on the outskirts of town. In town, there were white-washed clapboard buildings, brick buildings, and a few log cabins. Some housed businesses like the newspaper, mercantile, shoe shop, tailor, dressmaker. Others were boardinghouses, hotels, and a few less reputable places to lodge. Saloons, a bank, a bookstore, restaurants. Prescott had everything they could ask for, with less crime and grime than his former home.

He spotted the sign for his business: J.W. Harrison & Co. He pulled the wagon to a stop in front of it. Victoria didn't wait for him to help her down, she was so eager to walk around.

"I like it, Papa. Can we go inside?"

He led her into the building.

"Uncle Dixon!" Victoria exclaimed when she saw Joshua's friend and business partner.

Dixon Pike rounded the corner from the counter and held his arms wide. Victoria ran to him, and he lifted her in an embrace and spun her around. Joshua's lips stretched into a large smile and his heart warmed.

"Pumpkin!" Dixon exclaimed as his dark eyes sparkled. He groaned and set her down. "You've grown since I saw you last. I'm not sure, but you might be too old for the gift I got you."

Victoria's eyes grew wide. "What is it?"

Dixon reached into his leather vest pocket and pulled out a strand of licorice. When she tried to take it, he tightened his grip.

"Please? I'm not too old for candy." She clasped her hands in front of her and swayed back and forth, lowering her head slightly. That look always melted Joshua's heart. He knew Dixon stood no chance.

"Alright." Dixon handed her the treat and pinched her cheek. "It's good to see you."

"Thanks, Uncle Dixon." She gave him another hug and darted around the counter to explore.

"Victoria!" Joshua called to her. She turned back toward him. "Don't go in the back room. You can look around the office but wait for me or Dixon."

She nodded and headed towards the office.

"Cap!" Dixon greeted him while pulling him into a bear

hug.

Joshua smiled. The nickname was short for "Captain". The two served together at Fort Goodwin many years ago. Dixon usually called him J.W. when they were at work to promote the brand, yet in personal moments he used the nickname.

"Dixon. You headed out on a run?"

"Not until tomorrow. Come on back."

Joshua looked around the room. The counter went the length of the room, except for a doorway at the far end of the building. He followed Dixon through it and down the hall to the office.

"I like the layout."

"Thought you would. Always did bug me that we didn't separate the office more from the customer facing area down in Tucson."

Joshua nodded. Victoria came up to him and ducked under his arm, sliding one arm around his waist.

"Can we see the storeroom?" she asked.

Dixon led the way.

The room across from the office was L-shaped and went all the way to the back of the deep building. Stacks of crates stood taller than him in the main area. The section behind the office was smaller. Joshua released his hold on his daughter and walked over to a miniature looking wagon.

"Is this it? The handcart that Perry designed?"

"The original. We've tweaked the design a bit for the second one, though the first is still very useful. The newer design can hold more weight."

Joshua leaned down and rubbed a hand along the smooth wood. He noticed the subtle differences between the two. The newer one had a wider wheelbase, larger metal wheels, and a wider bed. Both looked sturdy and sure.

"He patent it yet?"

Dixon shook his head.

"He should. He deserves to get credit for this design. Then he could start selling them to other outfits, farmers, ranchers, storekeepers, and the like. He around?"

Dixon rubbed his bearded chin. "He's got the day off to spend with his missus and her son. But I'll talk to him about your idea. With a new family to support, the extra money would come in handy."

Joshua laughed. "We are paying him well aren't we?"

"'Course."

"Great job with the place. Couldn't be happier," Joshua said.

"Thanks, Cap."

"Now," he said turning toward his daughter, "let's see if we can't find our new house and get our things unloaded."

Dixon went out back to get Smalley and Ira before meeting Joshua out front.

"That all you brought?" Dixon asked.

"Yeah. I left the old house mostly furnished at the buyer's request."

Dixon shook his head. "Smalley, bring the wagon. The rest of us can walk."

Joshua's lips turned up on one side. Smalley was a huge man. Shoulders nearly as wide as the wagon seat and muscles that stretched his shirt taut in several places. They would make quick work unpacking his meager possessions.

"The place is only a few blocks from here," Dixon said.

Victoria placed her hand in Joshua's as they followed along beside Dixon. Within a few minutes they turned down a side street then crossed it and turned east towards the slope of a hill dotted with many houses. When they reached the top, Dixon turned north and stopped in front of a yellow painted two-story house. The porch was large enough for two chairs and a small table, though presently empty. The corners of the white porch posts boasted fancy scrollwork corbels.

"Used to be Judge Stanton's home before he married. It's been rented out several times over the years, though the last renters moved out a few months ago. The judge would be happy to sell it if you decide you like it," Dixon explained. "I hired a young local gal, Miss Bethie Larson, to come clean it and get it ready for you. She did a right fine job and would make a good housekeeper and nanny."

Joshua let out a slow breath as they stepped inside the home. The parlor was bigger than he expected. Lightly stained wood floors. Tall fireplace on the interior wall. Large windows on the front wall let in light from the sunny day.

Victoria stood in the center of the room. She tilted her head back and raised her arms out and spun around in circles. When she stopped, she giggled. Joshua laughed. He loved his little girl so much. She was fun and free, untainted by the tragedies that haunted him. She was too young to remember.

"I love it, Uncle Dixon!"

Dixon showed them the rest of the house. There was a small dining room off the kitchen. He would build a table that could seat six or eight. There was a room on the first floor across from the kitchen and next to the mud room.

"Might be a room for the housekeeper."

Joshua nodded.

The second floor held three bedrooms and a washroom. The room next to the washroom was the largest and would be his. Victoria already chose the one across from it facing the front of the house.

"Look Papa! Running water!" she exclaimed as she turned on the faucet of the sink in the washroom.

Joshua quirked an eyebrow as he looked at Dixon.

"Judge Stanton is a wealthy man. Made a good bit of money on mining in the early days. He's invested in many mines and local businesses in the area. He brought a man in from San Francisco to plumb this house and his newer home. Only a handful of businesses and homes have running water."

Joshua smiled. He and Victoria would enjoy the luxury.

They returned downstairs where Smalley and Ira set several crates. Joshua and Dixon helped while Victoria watched. In thirty minutes, the wagon was unloaded.

Dixon slapped him on the shoulder. "Think you could use a bit more furniture, Cap."

"Yeah, I was planning on looking around town to see what's available. Not looking forward to sleeping on the floor."

"You can share my bed, Papa."

"Thanks, Pumpkin, but it's a little small for my long legs."

He said his farewells to Dixon, Smalley, and Ira. He unpacked a few things so they would have light later in the evening to unpack the rest. Then he took Victoria to the furniture store, and they picked out a new bed for him, a couch and two chairs for the parlor and a small table for the kitchen that would double as a dining table until he made a larger one. The storekeeper offered to deliver the purchases for an extra fee which Joshua gladly paid. Then they stopped at the mercantile to pick up some food.

Within the hour, the new furniture arrived. Victoria unpacked their dishes and kitchenwares while he took the trunks of their clothes upstairs. He still needed a dresser for himself and Victoria. Selling much of their furniture with the old house made it easier to travel since he only needed one wagon. He was glad he did it, even though it would take some time to fully furnish their new home.

He came back downstairs and surveyed the kitchen and parlor. He was glad he brought his daughter there. He liked it already and she seemed too as well.

CHAPTER 5

"Papa!" Victoria shouted shaking Joshua from his sleep. "You were yelling."

His clothes were soaked, and his mouth felt sticky and dry. The room was dark, so he lit a lamp. It was two in the morning.

"I'm sorry, Pumpkin," he said. He thought maybe the nightmares would go away once they moved to a new home. "Did I frighten you?"

"No, Papa. I was just worried. You sounded scared."

He wrapped her in his arms. She leaned her head against his chest while he stroked her hair.

"Are you alright?" she asked him.

"I will be."

He kissed the top of her head and released her. "Go back to bed."

She slid from his bed and returned to her own.

He stood and closed the door. Then he wiped a hand over his face wondering what he may have said or screamed in his sleep. It had been months since his last episode. To have another one on their first night there was very disappointing.

Grabbing the glass from his nightstand, he went to the washroom to fill it from the sink. He chugged it then refilled the glass and returned to his room.

His damp pajamas clung to his skin, so he stripped down to his underwear before sliding under the covers again. Then he turned off the lamp and stared at the ceiling for a good hour before falling asleep again.

The next morning, Joshua rose and washed up in the washroom. He could really get used to the indoor plumbing. He dressed in a simple white button-down shirt and tan trousers with suspenders. Then he went downstairs and found the skillet and ingredients for pancakes.

Victoria's footfalls sounded above him. A few minutes later she appeared in her nightgown.

"Morning."

She yawned and dropped into one of the chairs at the table. She rested her head on the table and mumbled something that could have been "good morning."

"Made you some pancakes," he said as he set a plate in front of her. He put the syrup on the table.

She lifted her head. She poured some syrup on the pancakes and waited for him to sit down. She lowered her head as he prayed. When he finished, she propped one arm on the table and leaned her head against it.

"Tired?" he asked between a bite of pancakes.

"Mmm. Hmm."

He smiled. "Are you glad you don't start school until Monday?"

She grunted.

The rest of the meal passed in silence. Joshua sent Victoria upstairs to wash up and get dressed while he washed the dishes, still marveling over the plumbing.

A knock sounded at the door. He dried his hands and set aside the dish towel before making his way to the front door.

"May I help you?" he asked the young woman. She wore

a brown work dress, and her blond hair was pulled back into a bun at the base of her neck. She smiled.

"My name is Miss Elizabeth Larson. But you can call me Miss Bethie. Dixon Pike told me to be here at eight o'clock sharp."

He glanced at the clock on the mantle. Five minutes till. He appreciated that.

When he made no move to let her in, she added, "He said you were looking for a housekeeper to care for the house and your daughter."

Joshua opened the door wider and motioned her into the parlor. They discussed his expectations of the job and agreed on a wage. He showed her to the room off the kitchen.

"Oh, this will be just fine." Her head bobbed up and down.

"Papa?"

"Back here," he called out. "Victoria, come meet Miss Bethie."

Victoria gave a small curtsy. "How do you do?"

Miss Bethie leaned down to eye level. "Most excellent, now that I've met you."

Victoria beamed.

Joshua liked Miss Bethie already.

"I have three sisters," Miss Bethie said. "One of them is married to a livery owner here in town. I was hoping it would be fine if I take an afternoon or evening off from time to time to visit with her and her family?"

"Absolutely," Joshua agreed. "As long as I'm in town, or if Dixon is in a pinch."

"My things are still over at her place. I didn't want to drag them all the way here if you decided I didn't meet your expectations."

He asked for the address and promised to pick them up

later in the day. Then he turned to Victoria. "Well, Pumpkin, it looks like I will be able to go into the office without you today. Can you show Miss Bethie around?"

"Yes, Papa."

He leaned down and pointed to his cheek. She kissed it and he gave her a hug. Then he left directions for Miss Bethie should she need him for anything.

Joshua placed his hat on his head and walked to the office. When he arrived, the team had already pulled out for the day, so he went to the back office and started looking through the paperwork. Looked like they were headed down to Ehrenberg to pick up supplies for the military.

The next few days Miss Bethie, Joshua, and Victoria fell into a routine. Miss Bethie rose early and woke Victoria for school. Then she made them breakfast. Joshua left for the office and spent the day familiarizing himself with their local customers. He reviewed the accounting ledgers and started thinking about ways to grow the business in Prescott and throughout central Arizona.

In the evening he returned to see Miss Bethie had everything under control. Victoria finished her homework at the table while Miss Bethie made them supper. They ate and then Victoria helped with the dishes. He went to the parlor and spent time with her, playing checkers or a card game or just talking over the day. When it was time for Victoria to go to bed, Miss Bethie oversaw everything before she spent the rest of the evening in her room. He sat in the parlor reading until he was tired.

Miss Bethie was an interesting young woman. She was a bit chattier than he expected. He found it annoying until he realized that she knew a great deal about the area people and businesses through her family connections. Her father was co-owner of the area's largest ranch, Colter & Larson

Ranch. Her second oldest brother ran a horse breeding and training operation located at the ranch. Her oldest sister was married to a man who owned one of the several liveries in town. They were close friends with the owner of Lancaster's Boardinghouse. The Colter family, a name which he remembered from his previous life in the area, recently opened a butcher shop in town. There were many more people that she spoke of in the few short days working for him.

The one part of his new life he found disturbing was the nightmares. They returned full force. Worse than they had been in years. Too many times he woke in a fit, hoping he had not screamed out and disturbed Victoria or Miss Bethie. Hopefully, Miss Bethie's room was far enough away that she would never hear him.

It was unsettling and embarrassing. He was a grown man. He served many years in the cavalry traveling all over the western part of the country. He helped establish Fort Whipple and the new government of the Arizona Territory by escorting the governor to many towns and settlements when he first arrived in the territory. He fought Indians. He hunted down rustlers. He protected settlers. Sometimes at great cost to himself.

He displayed unwavering courage over and over again in his life. Yet, here he was out of the military for nearly seven years, a prominent businessman in the territory with freight hubs in Prescott, Tucson, Arizona City, and most recently Phoenix. As more and more people came, his business grew.

Joshua didn't understand why these nightmares plagued him at a time where he felt more settled and safer than ever before. It made no sense and he prayed they would stop and leave him in peace.

CHAPTER 6

A week after the funeral, Grace decided it was time to move on. She had a storeroom full of food, clothing, blankets, and medical supplies waiting to be delivered to the Yuman-Apache Indians living on the Camp Date Creek reservation located a few hours south of Prescott. It was time to resume her charitable efforts.

She squared her shoulders and looked through her closet. Daddy would not mind if she stopped wearing black. It might even help him start to move past his own grief. Her fingers rested on a sky-blue dress with a high neckline edged in cream lace. She particularly liked the hat that went with it, so she pulled the dress from the closet and laid it out on her bed.

After she finished washing up and brushing her hair, she put the dress on and looked in the mirror. As she smoothed the wrinkles out with her hands, she smiled at how the dress brought out the bluer flecks of color in her eyes. She pinned a black and ivory cameo at the center of the neckline. She coiled her long blond hair high on her head and secured the lovely blue hat with cream lace in place with a few hat pins.

When she went downstairs, she searched each room until she found Daddy in his study. She watched him from the doorway for several minutes. He stared out the window across from his desk with his hands limply resting on the top. His shoulders sagged. Her heart ached seeing how hard he took Mama's death. Maybe she should delay her trip.

No, she needed to get those supplies out to the starving children on the reservation. Daddy would survive, but they might not.

"Morning, Daddy," she said softly.

"Morning, sweetheart." He motioned her over for a hug.

"I miss her," he whispered. "I loved our conversations each morning when I brought her breakfast. She listened to me dream about new business opportunities and never complained that I bored her. She challenged me when I was wrong. She encouraged me and helped me learn how to be a father to you."

She kissed the top of his head and released the hug.

"I don't know what to do without her."

"I'm sorry, Daddy."

She stood in silence for several minutes trying to decide if she should stay to comfort him a little while longer or not.

"I'm sorry, sweetheart. You look like you were on your way out."

"I can stay if you want."

"No, don't let me keep you from your plans."

She smiled. "I'm headed to the Women's Aid Society. I need to finalize some things. I will likely be traveling down to Camp Date Creek on Thursday. Will you be fine?"

He nodded. "Tomorrow? You go on. Kingsley will make sure I have anything I need. Just let me know if your plans change."

She agreed. Then she left and walked several blocks to the J.W. Harrison & Company office. The teamsters at the freight office always helped her deliver any of the donations the Women's Aid Society collected.

Her work with the organization gave her purpose. They

raised money for specific causes, like when a local farmer's wagon broke and he could not afford a new one, they purchased one for him. The women also organized and hosted most of the town gatherings, such as the Independence Day celebration last month. The events were free to the public, but she insisted they take donations of food, clothing, blankets, and other goods for their local community and for the Indians at Camp Date Creek. As the President, it was her responsibility to see each event and charitable endeavor completed.

The donations from the Independence Day celebration waited on her to distribute them almost five weeks after the event, much longer than normal. She felt guilty for the delay. Mama had taken a turn for the worse the week after the event, so Grace stayed by her side. Then there were a series of dinners in support of Alex's political efforts. By the time her schedule freed up, Mama passed, and her attention diverted to a funeral instead of delivering the goods.

When Grace stepped into the freight office, she did not see Ira at the counter, so she rang the obnoxious cowbell. She found it annoying, but it seemed like the teamsters could hear the thing even when working in the back storeroom.

"Ira," she said when she heard footsteps down the hall. "It's Grace. I'm here about shipping…"

A tall man, who was most definitely not Ira, appeared from the back. My what wonderful blue eyes. They sparkled and reflected the light. Such a nice contrast to his lightly tanned skin. He was thin but still well built. His wavy light brown hair flopped over part of his forehead. A dimple in his chin added to his handsome appearance that nearly stole her breath away. When he smiled, she let out a quick breath and willed her heart to stop slamming into her chest.

"I don't believe we've met," she said, trying to recover. "I'm Grace Talbert."

His smile dimmed. "I'm sorry for your loss."

She glanced down at her dress. No, it was the blue dress she wore, the same blue as his amazing eyes.

He cleared his throat and rushed to explain. "I saw you. The funeral."

"You," she whispered. The man in the wagon who passed by. She looked away. "Mama was sick for a long time. She's at peace now."

"I'm so sorry," he said softly. He waited a few seconds before he smiled and said, "It's nice to meet you, Miss Talbert. I'm J.W. Harrison."

Her gaze traveled back to his eyes. Her eyes widened. "*The* J.W.? The one on the sign?" She pointed a finger up towards where she imagined the sign to be.

He laughed. "Yes, that very one. Though you may call me Joshua."

She smiled. "And you may call me Grace."

"How may I help you?" His gaze remained fixed with hers.

She touched her hair as her cheeks warmed. Words stuck in her throat. She gave a dainty cough into her gloved hand, hoping to find her words again.

"I work with the Women's Aid Society. We've gathered a large number of donations for Camp Date Creek at our building. Normally, I work with Ira or Dixon. They give us good pricing as we are a volunteer organization and receive only meager financial donations that barely cover the cost to ship goods."

Joshua nodded. "Do you know how many crates there are? Will you need crates for packing the goods?"

Grace set one hand on the counter and leaned forward

slightly mesmerized by those eyes. She nervously drummed her fingers on the counter. "Ira usually comes by and tells me what to do."

He stepped through the doorway adjacent to the counter and joined her in the waiting area. "I'm free if you'd like to show me."

Would she ever. Heat warmed the apples of her cheeks as she placed her hand in the crook of his arm as they exited the building. He stood roughly eight inches taller than her. He smelled like spice and musk. As they walked, she thought how much she liked being close to him.

If Alex Glassman had stirred such a response from her, she never would have broken off that relationship.

CHAPTER 7

Joshua swallowed hard when the woman from the funeral appeared across the counter from him. She was even more beautiful up close. The sky blue of her dress brought out the blue in her eyes which were surprisingly bright for having attended a funeral just days ago. Her lips were pink and full. Though she wore a hat, he still noticed how golden and shiny her blond hair looked.

He offered his arm. When her hand rested on the crook of his arm, fire shot through his veins at her touch. She smelled like lilacs on a summer breeze.

Joshua coughed and followed her lead to the Women's Aid Society. Once they arrived, she dropped her hand and led him through the front door all the way to the back of the building. When she opened the storeroom door, his jaw went slack.

"That's more than I expected."

"Oh." Her shoulders sagged. When her smile faded, he wanted to do whatever it took to see it again.

"Not to worry," he quickly added. "We can work with this."

Joshua tore his eyes off her as he walked along the stacks of crates. Looked to be two crates deep three crates wide and three crates tall. They could use the smaller wagon instead of one of the large freight wagons. He lifted the lid of one.

"Are they all as well packed as this one?"

Grace smiled and his heart flipped. "Ira trained me well."

He chuckled. "Glad to hear it."

"One more thing," she said. "I will be accompanying the goods. The Agent of Indian Affairs and I have an arrangement. When I bring the supplies for the Yuman-Apache, he assigns a soldier to help while I administer basic medical assistance to any of the Indians who are sick or in need."

Joshua tightened his jaw as his breath shallowed. He fisted his hand and squeezed until his knuckles turned white.

"Absolutely not." There was no way he was going to take her into a reservation full of Indians. He knew first hand how dangerous it was.

Grace took a step back. "What do you mean? Ira and I have made the trip twice before now."

"Ira is out on a run and won't be back for a week or more. You're stuck with me and there is no way I'm agreeing to that." He frowned and crossed his arms over his chest. The foolish woman had no idea how lucky she had been to come away unscathed if she had really been down there as many times as she led him to believe.

She frowned and lifted her chin. Her foot tapped a steady rhythm. "Why not?"

"Because I don't help Indians." Her safety was not the only reason behind his stubbornness. He suffered at their hands more than she could possibly comprehend.

She sucked in a loud gulp of air. Then she stepped closer and narrowed her eyes. "You won't? Or J.W. Harrison & Company won't?"

"I won't." He pressed his lips together in a firm line. No way was he letting her put herself in such danger.

She let out a frustrated groan. "We have been working

with your company for years on several similar projects. But *you* won't help those who are starving, cold, and sick?"

She paced back and forth periodically looking at him.

He closed his eyes and took a deep breath.

"Look," he said after a few minutes. "You have no idea what they did to—"

"I know good and well what many Indians have done. I also know what many whites have done to the Indians. These people are *starving!* They are forced to live on the reservation, but the new Indian Agent, Josephus Williams, refuses to feed them anymore. They aren't allowed to find food like they have for centuries because they are forced to live there!"

Joshua's blood boiled. She was insane if she thought he would agree to such nonsense. He walked out of the storeroom and headed for the front door with heavy footsteps.

"Wait!" she called after him. Her voice softened as she reached for his arm. "I'm sorry I lost my temper."

He snorted but turned to face her. "The most I will agree to, is to take the goods down there and drop them off. If you want to ride along then so be it. But once the crates are unloaded, we are turning around and coming right back here."

Her mouth opened and closed several times. At length she finally said, "That would be fine. Can we leave first thing in the morning?"

He nodded and stormed out of the building.

The absolute nerve of that woman! She had no idea what she was asking him to do or how painful it would be for him.

His heart squeezed. Victoria lost her mother because of Indians. He had so many deep scars from the abuse he suffered at their hand. Why would he want to help them?

To think he was attracted to her. That was just like him. Always falling for the proverbial damsel in distress. First Hannah. Then Rachel. In both cases these women needed his help. With his strong sense of duty and loyalty mixed with his compassion, he felt compelled to rescue them.

When Hannah's husband died, Joshua knew he had to help her. Her husband was his friend. His loyalty to him is what drove him to see her safely settled in Prescott. Only during the process, he lost his heart to a woman who could never love him.

Rachel. That was a complex situation. One that still felt too raw even after seven years. She saved his life. In return, he tried to help her. His heart became entangled, and his love went unrequited. He sometimes let his mind wonder about Rachel, if she would have come to love him had her life not been cut short. Not that it mattered. He was helpless to stop it.

Grace's desire to help others would normally be something he admired. But her charitable efforts were misplaced if she thought she could really help the Indians. They were a brutal people. He had seen with his own eyes the horror they were capable of inflicting.

Joshua entered the freight building and headed back to his office, thankful that Smalley was out on a local delivery. He was in no mood to be around people. He sat down at the desk and sighed heavily. He rubbed his hands through his hair. Then he rested his head in his hands as he propped his elbows on the desk.

When Grace spoke about the Indians, the passion in her eyes ignited. Had her words been about any other subject matter, he would have gladly agreed to any terms. Unfortunately, she was obviously determined to help the people that destroyed his and Victoria's lives. He could not afford to let his heart be ensnared by Grace, no matter how much he was drawn to her. He had his daughter to care for and his business to run.

He would take her freight down to Camp Date Creek and drop it off. Then he would take her back to Prescott and avoid her no matter what.

CHAPTER 8

Grace donned a practical brown dress with a high collar and long sleeves. It was the least flattering of her dresses and made her feel frumpy and plain. But it was the most practical choice for a long journey followed by a day in the dusty outdoors. She placed the serviceable straw hat on her head. It was a gift from Belinda, an area farmer's wife who helped at the last event. She said that Grace would need something more practical to keep the sun off her porcelain skin while she helped the Indians on the reservation.

She looked at the clock in her room. She was going to be late, so she rushed down the stairs and into the kitchen. Esther handed her a basket of food.

"I packed two lunches for you and the driver as well as some meat and cheese. You won't need to eat at that dirty dining hall at the fort if you don't want to."

"Thanks Esther," she said knowing full well she would eat the dreadful food at the dining hall and give away most of the delicious food in the basket to the starving children. She could survive eating a poor meal from time to time or even skipping a meal.

Grace headed toward the door which Kingsley opened for her.

"He's already gone on business, Miss Grace."

"Please take care of him while I'm gone. If I'm not back

late tonight, then I should be back by tomorrow evening."

"Miss Grace." Kingsley nodded.

Her feet pounded out a steady pace on the board side-walk as she hurried to the Women's Aid Society's building. When she arrived, she walked around back and found Joshua leaning against a wagon with arms crossed and deep creases in his forehead.

"You're late."

His terse greeting unnerved her.

"I'm..." She fumbled with her keys and dropped them. "Sorry."

He bent over and picked them up.

"It's the one with the blue ribbon."

He found the key and unlocked the door. She could feel his annoyance, so she followed him into the building.

"So sorry," she said breathlessly. Any excuse she could think of died on the tip of her tongue when he glared at her.

Joshua cleared his throat and let out a slow breath. "You can put that," he said pointing to the basket, "behind the wagon seat."

"Smalley couldn't wait," he growled, "so bear with me while I load everything."

He was upset with her. She glanced at the clock on the wall. Nine o'clock. She was late. An hour late. It was so un-like her, and she felt ashamed. She had overslept after lying awake for hours missing her mama.

He grunted as he lifted the first crate.

"I can help," she offered trying to find a way to smooth things over.

Joshua snorted. "Not likely. Step aside."

She flattened herself against the wall as he walked past her with the crate. She caught a whiff of spice and musk again. It must be his shaving soap. Her heart thrummed faster as she watched him walk out the door.

Heat warmed her entire face as she followed him. She rounded the wagon, careful to stay out of his way, and placed the basket behind the wagon seat as he instructed.

A half hour passed before the wagon was loaded. Joshua wiped his sleeve across his forehead. She held out a glass of water as a peace offering which he took and drained before handing the empty glass back to her.

"Help me with this tarp," he said when she returned from the kitchen.

He threw a tarp across the bed of the wagon.

"Do we really need that?" she asked.

"Grab the other end and hold it while I tie this side down. And yes," he barked, "we do need it. In case you haven't noticed we are in the middle of monsoon season. If we get caught in a downpour, you will thank me for it."

Grace held the other end of the tarp and pursed her lips into a thin line. He hated her. She was positive of it.

When they first met yesterday, she thought he might feel the same attraction that she had. But his curt words and stuffy demeanor could not be entirely from her tardiness, could it?

He finished tying down the one side of the tarp and he rounded the wagon and tied down the other side.

"Let's go," he said. Not bothering to help her up, he climbed onto the wagon seat.

No matter. She was an independent woman. She lifted her chin and hiked up her skirt with one hand. With the other, she reached for the edge of the wagon seat. Then she balanced one foot on a spoke of the wagon wheel and pushed up. She landed awkwardly in his lap, knocking her hat off center. Her hand accidentally grazed his thigh. She moved it but not before she noticed how incredibly strong it felt. Her cheeks burned as she scooted over to a proper place.

She straightened her hat and apologized for a third time. She hoped the day would get better.

He slapped the reins down on the horses' backs and they jerked forward. When the wagon shifted, she slid into his side. The touch sent tingles throughout her body. She breathed deeply and caught that musky spice smell. It turned her stomach in knots.

He frowned at her and slid over to the edge of the wagon seat again. As the wagon climbed up the hill out of town, she was convinced that any pleasantness he had shown her yesterday would probably not reappear today. Something about her request to take these goods to the Indians had cooled his perception of her.

When he pulled out his pocket watch he sighed heavily. "I thought you said you would be here first thing."

"I know, I'm sorry," she apologized yet again.

"It's going to be afternoon before we arrive there. By the time we unload everything, we'll be headed up the mountain at dusk. That's not good. It's a dangerous road."

She started to apologize again then stopped. It did not matter what she said. He hated her. Nothing she said would change that.

CHAPTER 9

Joshua caught that same fragrance from her when she landed on him getting into the wagon. Lilac. He breathed deeply of it then immediately chastised himself. He could not afford to have feelings for the woman no matter how beautiful she was.

Once they were out of town, tall pines lined both sides of the road casting shadow over them and the road. The forest seemed quiet. Maybe she would be too.

"Why do you hate the Indians so much?"

So much for quiet.

"Why do you like them?" he growled through gritted teeth.

She huffed and he quirked up one side of his mouth. He enjoyed goading her.

"Do you not believe our Constitution where it says that all men are created equal?"

"Yes, all men are created equal," he conceded wondering where she was going with that argument.

"Are the Yuman-Apache not men?" she baited.

"Look," he said as his nostrils flared. "They are not citizens of this country. They are not entitled to the same rights as you or me."

He clenched his jaw growing weary of her.

"I was once not a citizen of this country, yet I am now."

Joshua glared at her. "What do you mean?" he asked, figuring he would regret it in a moment.

"I was born in London."

"Don't sound like it," he said as they started down the switchbacks of the mountain.

"Whether I sound like it or not it is true. I was born in London. We emigrated to San Francisco when I was five. I was not born a citizen but became a citizen. So, could not the Indians become citizens, too?"

He grunted and kept careful watch on the horses as the road narrowed. When it widened again, he remained silent and hoped Grace would too.

"Are you a God-fearing man, J.W.?"

He narrowed his eyes. He didn't like her calling him that. It rankled him. "Joshua."

"Are you?"

"Yes."

"Does Jesus command us to love our neighbor and to care for the poor, the oppressed, widows, and orphans?"

He gritted his teeth. He was doing just that. His daughter was an orphan for goodness's sake. What did that have to do with the Indians?

Grace did not wait for his response. "The Indians are the poor and the oppressed. There are many starving children. You can see their rib cages and sunken bellies. You will see when we get there."

The wagon rocked over a bump in the road, causing him to slide into her side. The fire that moved from his hip to his heart threw him off kilter. She was so blasted annoying and amazing all at the same time.

"I have half a mind to turn this wagon around when we get to the bottom of this mountain," he threatened.

"But you won't," she said as she lifted her chin.

"What makes you so sure?" he challenged her. He wanted to hear why she thought he was bluffing.

"You are a man of character and principle. I sensed that at the funeral and in your office."

He moaned low and guttural. She was right, though he had no idea how she knew it.

They reached the bottom of the mountain. The road flattened out and the horses seemed to relax as they plodded along the grasslands. A large rock jolted the wagon followed by a creak and a very loud snap. The wagon came to a stop and tilted suddenly, throwing Grace to the ground. Dang it.

He pulled back on the reins and set the brake before jumping down.

"Are you alright?" he asked as he took her arm to help her to her feet. The touch sent his pulse racing again.

She laughed nervously. "I think so," she said as she brushed bits of grass from her skirt and straightened her hat. She rubbed her right wrist.

His gut tightened. Better not be broken. That was the last thing he needed.

"Let me see." He took her hand in his and tried to pretend there were no currents running up his arm. He turned her hand over and pressed his fingers all over her hand. When he pressed on the outside of her wrist she winced.

"Can you move it?"

Grace rotated her wrist.

"Does it hurt?" He held his breath.

"No."

He let out his breath. "Good. Probably not broken."

Joshua stepped away from her and was relieved when the sparks in the air between them settled. He turned and inspected the wagon. Several spokes of the wheel were split. He kneeled on the ground, then laid on his side and inspected under the wagon. The axle splintered and it was not safe to continue. He cursed under his breath.

When he jumped up to his feet, he scanned the horizon. They were too far away from any of the area ranches to walk. He glanced back up the mountain and shook his head. Some fine mess they were in.

"How bad is it?" Grace asked.

He walked around to the other side of the wagon and lifted the lid on his supply box. He cursed at himself. Foolish. He had been so annoyed that she was late that he forgot to double-check the box before he left. No slickers for when it rained. No clamps to patch an axle. No mallet. No wrench. No spyglass to see what was in the distance. No blankets. Just a shovel, extra flint, everything to make coffee, and some extra ammunition for his rifle and revolver.

"Not good," he finally admitted, kicking himself for his stupidity. "I'm not going to be able to repair this."

Even if he could, the most he could hope for was getting to the remains of a ranch he noticed on the way in last week. They would be at the mercy of whoever came along whether they stayed where they were or tried to continue.

Someone would come along; he was certain of that. It was a well-traveled road. Freighters, express riders, ranchers, the military, and even private citizens all used the road to get to Prescott and Fort Whipple. In a day or two someone would rescue them.

A day or two. With her. With those beautiful eyes and pert lips. With her perfect shape and incessant questions. He swallowed hard.

Grace stepped in front of him and looked up. Her eyes were wide, and she grabbed his arms. "What do we do?"

He closed his eyes and took a deep breath. Pressure. He thrived under it. She was counting on him to rescue her, and he would do his best not to let her down.

CHAPTER 10

Grace's breaths came in short puffs. Joshua said he could not fix it. She had traveled the road enough to know how sparsely populated it was. They were hours away from the nearest ranch, except maybe the burned out remains of Perry Quinn's old place. Though it was the only route between Prescott and the valley and destinations further south, it could be days before anyone came along.

She was brave enough to walk into a camp of several hundred Yuman-Apache, but the thought of being stranded in the grasslands terrified her.

"Grace." His voice was soft and soothing. He rubbed his hands up and down her arms leaving a trail of warmth behind.

She looked up at him. His eyes were soft. His face confident.

"We'll figure this out."

She shivered despite the hot sun beating down on her back.

"Trust me."

Trust him. She did not know him. All she knew was that he owned a freighting company. She thought back to when he passed by the funeral. A young girl sat next to him. He had a daughter. Surely, she could trust him.

She let out a slow breath and nodded.

"Good. Tell me what's in that basket of yours."

She pulled it from behind the wagon seat. "I know Esther packed food and water this morning."

He stood behind her so close she caught the spicy smell of him. Her heart raced faster as she opened the basket.

"Four sandwiches. Two large jars of water. Dried meat, cheese, and some dried fruit. Two forks and knives. Goodness! She must be convinced I am not eating enough since Mama passed."

He reached around her to open the other side and his arm brushed against hers. She felt lightheaded.

His deep voice reverberated in her ear. "Napkins."

He laughed. "Was she expecting us to stop for a picnic?"

When he moved away, she finally found her voice. "I suppose so."

"Don't suppose there's a large metal clamp or wrench in there."

Grace laughed as her breathing returned to normal. She dropped the lid back into place. Then she turned to face him. "No. Nothing more useful than sustenance."

He lifted his hat and ran his hand through his hair. "We've got a few choices."

She nodded and hoped he had a plan.

"We can go find water for the horses and ourselves, bring the basket of food, shovel, and flint and try to find firewood to make a camp."

"That's the first choice?"

He nodded. "Or we can stay here near the road and the wagon to wait for someone to come along. But if we do that, we eventually have to find some water for the horses, even though we have enough for ourselves today."

"What about walking on towards Quinn's old ranch?" she asked.

He shook his head. "If I remember correctly, it is a good ten to fifteen miles away. Best case we could unhitch the horses and ride there, but we don't know what we'll find. No one will look for us there. If we stay relatively close to the wagon, anyone who comes along will see us or the horses and stop to investigate. At least that's what I'd do."

Grace's eyes burned. Their situation was overwhelming. She missed her mama. Her daddy would be worried sick. She had no idea how long they would be stranded. It could be hours. It could be days. Her stomach twisted in knots.

Joshua closed the distance to her and pulled her into his arms as her tears fell. He stroked her back leaving warm tingles behind. She wrapped her arms around him and leaned her head against his chest, letting her tears fall. The warmth of his arms around her felt comforting.

After several minutes she pulled away.

"I'm sorry," she said as she wiped away the tears with her handkerchief. "It's been a long week."

"We'll make it through this. I promise."

She studied his eyes. His shoulders were back and his posture perfectly straight. It reminded her of the cavalry riders at the Independence Day celebration. Confident and calm.

"Let's unhitch the horses and walk them over to that area." He pointed to a small cluster of trees about the same distance as walking from her home to the church. "Do you see where there is a line across the grass that is in shadow?"

Grace nodded.

"I think that is water."

"I... Don't know how to unhitch horses."

He chuckled. "Then it's a good thing I do. Why don't you bring the basket and I'll bring the horses? If nothing else, we can eat lunch in the shade."

She grabbed the basket and hung the handles on her arm. She watched as Joshua unclipped and unbuckled several straps. Within a few minutes the horses were free, and he held the reins in his hands causing the horses to follow behind them.

"How are you so calm?" she asked as they walked.

"I served in the First Cavalry from '61 to '65."

She smiled. Of course, he was former cavalry. It explained his need for punctuality.

"Were you in the war between the states back East?"

"No. I was part of the Army of the West. Traveled all over Kansas, Colorado, New Mexico, Arizona, and parts of California."

"So, this is very familiar to you."

"Yes, though, being accompanied by one idealistic woman versus a company of smelly dirty men is nice."

She laughed as her face warmed.

They covered the distance quickly. She was impressed when they neared the shadowy line. It was a creek as he suspected.

Grace set the basket next to the tree while he led the horses to the water. The creek was fast moving but shallow. She could see rocks and pebbles at the bottom. It was about twenty feet wide.

She inched her way down the steep bank. Her foot caught on something, and she landed face first in the stream.

"Grace!"

Joshua ran from nowhere and scooped her up in his arms. Her heart pounded loudly in her ears as he carried her back up the bank. She felt dizzy. When he lowered her legs to the ground, he did not release her. Her hand slid from his neck down his chest. He took her hand and slid it back up to his neck but not before she noticed a lump beneath his shirt that felt like a nasty scar.

She looked up and studied his face as her pulse quickened. The stubble of his beard left a light shadow. His chin dimpled. His cheeks were flush. Those blue eyes searched hers before she dropped her gaze to his lips.

"Grace." He moaned and captured her lips in his.

Warmth spread over her body, and she clasped her hands behind his neck. He deepened the kiss searching and probing. He stirred something in her that she never felt before, but she liked it and returned his kiss with equal fervor. Her fingers traced his hairline at the back of his neck, and she leaned into him savoring the way he explored her mouth.

His hands pressed her closer. His strong body felt amazing against her. She matched his intensity as his hands moved across her back to her waist. The hunger in her soul surprised her and she welcomed it.

CHAPTER 11

Joshua groaned when Grace responded to his kiss. She pressed her body closer to his and he felt like she belonged there. His hands studied every inch of her back and waist before moving up to her neck. While he kissed her, he flung her hat to the ground and touched her hair. It was as silky as he imagined.

She responded with ardency and his heart raced. She stoked a desire in him unlike any other. Her fingers touched the edge of his hair on the back of his neck. Then she traced his jawline. When a soft moan came from his throat, he realized he need to get control of himself before he lost all his senses.

He slowed the kiss. Then he rested his forehead against hers, unwilling to release her from his arms just yet. His breath came in ragged spurts as he closed his eyes.

Grace's hands released from behind his neck and slid down his chest. Her touch made him want her more. He had to put some distance between them, or he did not know what he might do. He captured her hands in his and stepped back. Then he released her hands and took another step back, trying to douse the fire that burned in him.

The look on her face. Oh, it stirred him. Her fingers touched her lips. She had never been kissed like that before. Well, he had never kissed a woman with such a lack of restraint. He was not entirely sure what came over him. But he liked it.

Joshua cleared his throat as his breathing steadied and his pulse slowed. A smile turned up one corner of his mouth. He wiggled his eyebrows. "Now that we've had dessert, maybe we should eat some lunch."

She puffed out a small breath but made no move toward the basket, so he did.

He took a seat, and he opened the basket. She still had not moved. He pulled out the first two sandwiches. "Looks like chicken salad," he said marveling that there was no crust on the bread. "And this one is ham."

Grace stirred and sat down on the ground with the basket between them. Her cheeks were rosy, and her lips were red. He tried to squelch the desire to kiss her again as she leaned against the trunk of the tree.

"Which would you like?" he asked.

She cleared her throat and tugged on the wet skirt of her dress to arrange it to fully cover her legs. Too bad. What he saw of them looked pleasing.

"Chicken."

He handed her the sandwich. Then he took a big bite of the ham sandwich. "Mmm. This is good."

Grace nibbled her sandwich.

He swallowed another bite. "You don't like the crust?"

She smiled. "When I was a little girl, I was fascinated with the finger sandwiches Mama served with afternoon tea. I wanted to eat the fancy sandwiches all the time. So, Esther, our cook, trimmed off the crust and served me 'fancy' sandwiches for lunch every day."

Joshua chuckled. "Well, your fancy ham sandwich is delicious."

They sat in silence as she finished her sandwich. The

horses ambled over so he stood and looped the reins over the branch of the tree. Then he sat down and leaned against the trunk.

When a light breeze tickled his neck, he glanced at the sky. A few clouds dotted the sky and cast long shadows over sections of the grasslands that spread out before them.

"Why do you hate Indians?" Grace asked softly.

"Grace," he warned as he frowned.

"I truly want to understand."

He sighed. She would not let it go so he should probably give her some answer. "I'll tell you if you promise to answer my question."

She nodded.

Joshua swallowed hard, carefully weighing how much to share.

"When I was stationed at Fort Goodwin in southeastern Arizona back in '65, my company patrolled the area around the Gila River. I was a captain then. Dixon, who I met at Fort Goodwin, was a sergeant.

"Many immigrants from Ireland settled near the river and farmed the land. We were near the end of our patrol zone when we spotted a band of Apache raiders. They attacked us and overwhelmed us. Only Dixon and I survived.

"Dixon was the luckier of us two. They thought he was dead, so they left him where he fell. He eventually came to and rode back to Fort Goodwin.

"I was not so lucky. They beat me, tortured me, and..." He swallowed hard as his skin crawled. "They took me back to their camp, stripped me naked and threw me in a deep dark hole."

Grace gasped and clutched a hand near her chest.

Joshua pressed on. "When I was almost dead, they pulled me up out of that pit and rode me to a farm and dropped my body on the doorstep of a widow. I firmly believe they thought I was dead and that it was a message for the widow to leave."

He glanced over at her. Her mouth was parted, and her eyes rounded.

"The widow was Victoria's mother, Rachel."

He looked down at his trousers and rubbed his hands on his legs, hoping to hide how they shook. He could still smell the silt and dirt from the pit. He needed to focus on something else.

"She's not my daughter, you know," he said at last.

"Victoria?"

He shook his head.

"She's Rachel's from before her husband was murdered by the same band of Apache. They terrorized her for years and never touched her. Not until they found out she nursed me back to life."

Joshua's breaths came in short bursts. His throat constricted. He needed to pull himself together. He could not fall apart in front of her. Not her. Not after that passionate kiss.

He coughed several times. Then he leaned his head back against the tree and closed his eyes. He took slow deliberate breaths. Lilac.

When he opened his eyes, she was right next to him. She had moved the basket to her other side. She took his hand between hers and held it.

"Anyway." He cleared his throat. "They murdered Rachel and on her dying breath she asked me to take Victoria as my own daughter."

He pulled his hand away and tried to laugh off his heaviness only it came out sounding more like a cackle. He stood and paced back and forth for a minute. She stayed seated.

He never told another soul most of what he just shared with Grace. Not even Dixon, though he was sure Dixon had pieced together most of it over time.

The memories of that time threatened to pull him to a place he did not want to go. The pit. The cold. The hunger. The bruises. The bugs crawling on his skin. His throat constricted. His stomach churned.

He reached down and grabbed one of the jars of water and took a long drink. *Get a hold of yourself, Joshua. Forget about it. Think of Victoria. Her smile. Her cute little freckles.*

Joshua set the jar down. He took off his hat and ran his hands through his hair. His daughter would worry when he failed to come home tonight. At least he had a dependable housekeeper to care for her and keep her calm.

"What did you want to ask me?" she said calmly.

He stuffed his hands in his pockets and stopped pacing.

"Why do you want to help the Indians so much?"

———

"Why do I want to help the Indians so much?" Grace repeated the question back to him.

Her heart hurt for Joshua and his story. She could tell it was not the full story, but it was enough to explain why he hated them. If she was honest, she could not fault him for it. She supposed if she suffered as terribly as he did, she would not help the Indians either.

"I do believe deeply that all men are created equal. I do believe that they have rights at a basic human level, whether or not the Constitution is ever applied on their behalf."

Joshua coughed.

"Please, Joshua, sit." She patted the ground next to her.

He hesitated a moment before sitting down.

"I also believe that God does ask us to help those less fortunate. I come from a wealthy family. Daddy is a shrewd businessman and has built a fortune."

She glanced away, then pulled her knees up to her chest and hugged them. Then she rested her chin on her arms. It had been so much easier to live a privileged life before she learned about the dark side of her father and his business dealings.

She lowered her voice. "I am not naive about some of the less savory ways my father has built his wealth. I fear some of my drive to help others comes from an overwhelming guilt for his actions. Or maybe it's that I'm trying to make up for the harm he causes. I don't know."

She sighed. She knew she was not responsible for her father's actions, but it did not keep her from feeling guilty anyway.

"I can't tell you how many suitors over the years have been afraid to break off a lack luster relationship with me out of fear of my father and his power."

She straightened her legs and leaned against the tree trunk. She gave a half-hearted laugh. "I'm left to break it off, so they don't suffer Daddy's wrath."

"The most perplexing thing about Daddy is that he deeply loves me and Mama. Loved. He loved her."

The pain of the loss of Mama washed over her. A tear slid down her cheek and Joshua reached over to wipe it away, his eyes full of compassion.

"I suppose I would rather have a father who is feared by the world and adores me, than one who is loved by the world and abuses me."

She never confessed these thoughts to a living soul, not even Mama. She was not sure why she chose to say them aloud to Joshua.

"Anyway. That's the crux of my odd family dynamics and my drive to save everyone."

He shifted closer and lightly ran his fingers along her cheek. Then he leaned in and kissed her. Softly. Kindly. Compassionately.

It was too brief.

The sky grew dark overhead. A loud clap of thunder echoed across the valley. Grace jumped. The clouds let forth a torrent of rain. The trees did little to cover them.

"Come on," he said. He grabbed her hands and pulled her to her feet. Then he held her hand as they ran back to the wagon. Large drops of rain pelted against them. She left her hat behind, and the water streamed down her face and neck.

"The horses!" she yelled over the loud hissing of the rain.

"They'll be fine."

When they reached the wagon, she stood shivering. She was soaked to the bone. He untied several sections of the tarp. Then he stacked a few crates on top of each other to create a space for them. He held up the edge of the tarp and motioned her in. Then he jumped in beside her.

She hugged her arms around her, and her teeth chattered. She was cold. The air must have dropped twenty degrees since the rain started to pour.

Joshua rubbed his hands up and down on her arms. The warmth of his touch caused her heart to race.

"Scoot closer."

She did. He kept rubbing her arms and back until her shivering stopped.

"You alright?"

A long deep rumble of thunder shook the wagon. She squealed and he held her tighter. His shirt stuck to his body, outlining every muscle.

From their vantage point under the tarp, they could see the horses in the distance. They raised and lowered their heads. They pranced in place, clearly disturbed by the violent storm.

The sky grew darker. It was difficult to tell if it was only because of the storm or because of the late hour.

"The food!" she exclaimed when she realized they left it.

"Hopefully Esther's basket is waterproof."

Another roll of thunder preceded streaks of lightening. A loud boom sounded directly above them. Grace buried her face against his slopping wet chest. She rubbed her hand over the spot she noticed before. She could clearly feel the marred skin from the scar.

"Grace," his voice was husky. "Don't."

He grabbed her wrist and gently moved her hand to her lap.

"Is that from…"

CHAPTER 12

Joshua swallowed hard. His heart raced at Grace's touch and her nearness. They were both cold and wet. It was for shared body heat that they clung to each other. At least that is what he told himself.

When she touched his chest, he was nearly undone. She was so young and naive. She could not possibly know how such an intimate touch stirred him. If he allowed himself to kiss her, he doubted he would be able to rein in his desire.

He took a shaky breath before he replied, "Yes. That scar is from the attack."

The space beneath the tarp was small. Too small. Dark and damp. No light. Too much like the pit where he only saw a small circle of sunlight each day. It had been so deep. No way to climb out. The bugs crawled on his skin. The places his skin had been ripped open oozed. Sharp pain stabbed him with each breath. He could not go back there.

His face warmed and perspiration dotted his forehead. His breaths came in short raspy waves. He shook. He did not want to go back there.

Dizziness clawed at him. His skin crawled. His vision blurred. He dug his nails into the palm of his hand. *Please God help me.* It had been the cry he uttered every hour of every day in that pit.

"Joshua." Grace's voice sounded far off. Distant.

Soft warm lips brushed his. Where was he? Who was that angel?

"Tell me about Victoria."

Grace. His chest heaved. His stomach churned. He needed out of the tight space. He rocked back and forth. His muscles tightened until they seemed like they would split.

A loud peal of thunder echoed around them. The rain pelted the top of the tarp with loud plops and splats.

He had to get out of there. His limbs felt heavy and immovable. His eyes darted to the opening. It was so dark.

"Joshua."

A hand slapped him hard across the face. His cheek stung. "Grace?"

"You're scaring me."

He rubbed his cheek. "I… Sorry."

She whispered, "Tell me about your daughter."

He nodded and felt like Grace was far away again. "She is…" He gasped for air. "Eleven."

"How old was she when you met her?"

"Three." He tried to fill his lungs with air. The space still felt like it was closing in. He closed his eyes. Images from the pit tried to take control.

"Joshua! Don't you dare leave me."

He took a slower breath and his throat opened again.

"How long has she been yours?"

"Seven." Deep breath. Eyes open.

"Years or was that her age?"

"Years." Slow. Air.

"What is she like?"

Air. Breathe. His pulse slowed down. Grace came into focus again. Tears rolled down his cheeks. His muscles slowly uncoiled.

"What is Victoria like?"

"She is fun." His breathing returned to normal. "I love her cute freckles."

He took a few more deep breaths and looked at Grace.

"How did you know?" He could not believe she knew exactly how to help him.

He could see her smile in the fading light. "Mama had consumption and would panic when she could not control the coughing. I learned that distracting her with something helped pull her out of the fear."

"You are full of surprises." He was embarrassed that she had witnessed him falling apart, yet grateful she pulled him back to reality.

She shrugged. "I know. Now tell me more about Victoria."

"She has this laugh. It is so free. She is fearless and bold. I suppose her parents had to have been to farm in such a dangerous area."

The rain slowed and he lifted the edge of the tarp. The cool fresh air filled his lungs and his muscles felt like jelly. It was too dark to see the horses. It was getting hard to see Grace.

Exhaustion overwhelmed him as it often did after such an episode.

"Grace?"

"Yes?"

"I need to sleep," he whispered as the last bit of energy faded from his body.

He shimmied down to let his feet hang over the edge of the wagon. Rain misted his ankles. She did the same and pressed against his side. Then sleep covered him in darkness.

———

Grace rested her head on Joshua's chest as it rose and fell softly. He slept, finally at peace after that horrible panic attack. It was good that he fell asleep. She realized too late how her touch stirred his passion. She could tell he fought against it.

Her mind raced. She liked lying there next to him no matter how improper it was. They were both soaked and cold and needed each other.

Was it only a week ago that she released Alex from their courtship because they had no spark, no connection?

It was the right decision. Even more so considering the attraction she and Joshua shared. She had no idea how good it could feel. She felt relieved that she had not ended up in a marriage without it.

Her cheeks warmed as she thought about his kiss earlier. So full of promise and desire. Her whole body warmed as she remembered how exhilarating his touch felt. She would welcome another kiss again.

Grace carefully sat up trying not to disturb Joshua. She touched her hair and realized what a mess it was. She found the few pins that remained and pulled them out. Then she draped her half damp half dry hair over her shoulder and used her fingers to comb it.

The sound of the rain stopped. She held her hand outside of the covering to confirm it. The cooler air gave her goose bumps and she shivered. She dropped the tarp back in place and sighed.

Her heart ached for Joshua and the trauma he suffered. She could hardly imagine what that would do to a person. She wished she had known that before she badgered him about why he hated them. She could not have known the deep pain that lied just under the surface.

Through most of the trip, he appeared calm and confident. He spoke so lovingly of his daughter, even though she was not his flesh and blood. In the few short days she had known him, she saw his character clearly. He was a good man.

She had no idea what the future would hold for them. The closeness they experienced that day would linger with her for some time.

Graced yawned and laid down again, turning her back to Joshua. Then she fell asleep listening to his soft breathing.

CHAPTER 13

Joshua woke the next morning to Grace's arm across his chest. Her golden hair was loose and tickled his arm. She felt good so close to him. What would it be like to wake her with another kiss?

He chastised himself and slowly eased out from under her arm. He needed to get his mind off her before he did something he would regret.

When he reached the bottom of the wagon, he ducked out from under the tarp and hopped down. He stood and stretched the stiffness out of his muscles. Dawn colored the sky with pink and coral stripes.

He walked over to the tree where the horses stood. He examined them, glad to see they weathered the storm. He grabbed the reins and led them down to the rushing creek for a long drink. When they had their fill, he led them back up near the tree.

Several small branches laid on the ground, so he gathered them, thankful they had dried. Then he took the wood to a spot near the wagon and dropped it in a pile. He opened the box behind the wagon seat slowly and retrieved the shovel, flint, coffee pot, mugs, and coffee.

With the shovel, he cleared a small section of grass away. Then he built a fire. Once it was going, he took the coffee pot down to the stream and filled it with water. Then he came back to the fire and got the coffee started.

His eyes scanned the area, and he found a small log nearby that would make a great makeshift bench. He dragged it over closer to the fire.

Taking a deep breath, Joshua let it out slowly. The sky started to turn blue as the sun rose.

So much happened yesterday. He fell in love with Grace in one day. One day with her. He was frustrated with himself. It seemed when he opened his heart to a woman it was all or nothing.

He wiped a hand over his face and sat down on the log. He had not done a good job of leading yesterday. He allowed his emotions and his attraction to lead himself and Grace into some pretty dangerous territory. He knew better than that.

For a man who claimed to love God and desire to follow the example Christ set, he failed miserably. Not once had he stopped to pray over their situation. He just plowed full speed ahead following his own plan and he swept Grace along with him.

He truly wanted to be a godly man. Yet, when he was faced with the most tempting situation, he acted without thinking or praying.

He did not even know if Grace was unattached. Never once did he think to ask. It was not like him to ignore propriety to the depths in which he had.

Thank goodness for his episode. Who knows what he would have done sleeping next to her like that? He owed her an apology.

He heard her stir and when she stepped out of the wagon, his breath caught. Even with a rumpled dress she looked stunning. Her blond hair hung down over one shoulder, shining like gold in the early morning light. He swallowed hard. He needed to get his attraction under control, especially if they were not rescued that day.

———

Grace woke as the sunlight spilled through the foot of the wagon. She felt next to her, but Joshua was gone. She stretched and pulled back the tarp. Not a cloud in the sky. The cool air smelled clean like the morning after a purifying rain.

She shimmied to the edge of the wagon and jumped down.

"Morning," Joshua said from behind her.

"Morning. You look well rested."

He snorted and handed her a steaming cup of coffee. She raised an eyebrow.

"I always bring coffee. Always." He smiled, his eyes sparkling with restrained laughter.

"Yes, but how did you make it?" she asked as she breathed in the rich aroma.

"With fire."

She took a sip, letting the bitter drink warm her.

"Come see."

He took her hand and led her a few feet away from the wagon to a large log that sat near the fire. He motioned to it.

"Have a seat."

She smiled. "How did you clear the grass?"

"One of the few things I did pack was a shovel."

She mouthed the word, "Oh." She sat down on the log and took another sip of the warm liquid.

"And the firewood?"

Joshua laughed. "Do you always ask so many questions

first thing in the morning?"

Grace shrugged.

"The storm downed a few smaller limbs from the tree near the horses. They are fine in case you were about to ask."

He took a seat next to her and poured some coffee in a second mug.

Even though her dress dried out overnight as she slept in it, the warmth of the fire was comforting.

She wondered how long before someone would find them. Would they be found that day? The next? How much food did they have left? She frowned.

"Grace," Joshua said angling toward her. "Would you mind if I pray?"

Her heart melted. She nodded and closed her eyes, wishing she thought of it.

"Lord, you know the details of our circumstance. I have no idea why you threw us together or why we are stranded here. We know you are faithful and will bring help in your timing. We rejoice in our sufferings because we know that you produce endurance in us through it. That endurance produces character and character produces real hope in your love. Give us courage this day to trust our situation to you. In Jesus' name. Amen."

"Amen," she whispered. A gentle peace swept her anxiety away.

"You hungry?"

Grace shook her head. The coffee was welcomed, but she preferred to ration whatever food they had left. She would be fine if they waited until later in the day to eat something.

"The meat and cheese in the basket look salvageable. I'm sorry to say your fancy sandwiches did not survive." He winked at her.

She smiled before taking another sip of coffee.

"My teamster food is as good as ever," he said sarcastically.

She giggled. "I take it teamster food isn't good on a normal day."

Joshua shrugged. "It calms a hungry stomach."

She stared into the fire. Peace settled around her heart. Joshua was right. These sufferings produced endurance and character. They would be found. They would survive.

He cleared his throat several times and she turned to look at him.

"I owe you an apology."

She frowned. She did not want him to apologize to her for his amazing kisses that ignited something deep within her soul.

"Hear me out. Yesterday, I was—still am—drawn to you. But I allowed myself to be carried away with that kiss. Those kisses. I—"

"Stop." She shook her head. "There is nothing to apologize for." She nudged him with her shoulder. "I rather enjoyed them."

"But I never asked your permission. I did not even ask if you were, um, courting anyone or…"

"I am not." She decided not to mention how recently she had been. No need to make him feel bad.

"Still, I should have behaved better."

"You did nothing wrong, so stop trying to apologize."

He looked down at the log and picked off a piece of bark before flicking it away.

"Joshua," she said. She did not like the thought of him feeling guilty. They managed not to cross any lines that she was not comfortable with. "There is no harm to my reputation. I appreciate that you showed restraint when it mattered the most. I am drawn to you, and I hope that when we get home safely, we might get to know each other better."

"You do?"

"Yes. Truly I do."

He smiled and it warmed her heart.

"Do you still think we should stay put?" she asked.

Joshua nodded. "We'll reevaluate this afternoon, though we did have a pretty good shelter last night."

They settled into silent waiting. For what, she did not know.

CHAPTER 14

Joshua stood and walked away from the fire. His eyes scanned the horizon for any sign of travelers. The storm last night probably made the roads a mess that morning. It could be several hours or even another day before anyone happened upon them.

The food situation would be a problem soon. He figured if they ate only one meager meal that day, they could save his teamster food for the next day. Unless he could hunt for a rabbit or quail. Though he did not see any animal signs so far.

He sighed heavily. They were in a fine mess. When she emerged from the wagon with her hair down, he struggled. He did not trust himself to be so close to her again. Not at night.

He kicked at a small rock. She witnessed the worst of him last night. He could not control his reaction in small, enclosed spaces. He knew it was from the abuse he suffered and the long days and nights in that pit. It did not matter how much he prayed; the attacks came without warning when the conditions were right. It was the thorn in his side.

Joshua walked over to check on the horses. He took the reins and led them to the water. While they drank their fill, he watched Grace.

Her mother picked the perfect name for her. She was

graceful. Classy and elegant that first day in his office. Passionate about helping others. Humble and kind that morning.

So much for not entangling his heart with another woman who needed rescued. Only Grace was different. That kiss. She was drawn to him as much as he was to her. Perhaps, when they got back to Prescott, something would develop out of their closeness. A part of his heart reluctantly hoped for it. His heart could not face rejection again.

Off in the distance he thought he heard a cowbell. He led the horses back to the shade of the tree and looped the reins over a branch. He strained to hear.

It did sound like the jangle of a cowbell and squeak of harnesses. He hurried back to the wagon.

"What is it?" Grace asked.

"Shh."

His eyes roved the horizon. In the distance he saw the unmistakable line of a twelve team of mules pulling a double wagon. They were headed toward them.

"Oh!" she exclaimed. She stood and waved her arms.

Joshua chuckled. "You can sit and wait. They have to go past us."

Pink colored her cheeks and she sat.

He emptied the basket and jogged back down to the creek. After he filled it with water, he brought it up and doused the fire. He used the shovel to toss dirt over any lingering embers. Then he stood next to Grace and wrapped his arm around her shoulders.

They watched and waited as the teamsters came ever closer. When he recognized Dixon, he released Grace.

"It's Dixon and Perry," he said.

She smiled.

Dixon jumped down as Perry set the brake.

"Cap, are you alright?" Dixon asked looking them both over.

"We are no worse for the wear."

"Miss Talbert," Dixon greeted.

Perry joined them and touched the tip of his hat in greeting. "Broken axle?"

"Yeah," Joshua said. "Forgot to pack the repair kit."

Dixon glanced at Grace. "I can see how you might forget."

Joshua rubbed a hand on the back of his neck.

"You full up?"

Perry nodded. "If two of us ride bareback on the horses, Miss Talbert can sit on the wagon seat. Otherwise, it'll be uncomfortable if not impossible to sit on the crates in back."

"But what about the supplies for Camp Date Creek?" Grace asked, pointing over her shoulder to the broken wagon.

"We'll have to leave 'em and come back for them tomorrow," Dixon replied.

Her shoulders sagged. Joshua wished he could do more, but Dixon was right. It made more sense to head up to Prescott with them and deal with the wagon and its cargo another day.

"I'll ride a horse," Perry volunteered.

"I'll take the other one," Joshua said. It would be rough, but he had ridden bareback on other occasions during his time with the Army.

Perry fetched the horses.

"This way, Miss Talbert," Dixon said.

———

Grace stared at the large wheels on the freight wagon.

There was no way she could climb up there.

"Here." Joshua crouched down and cupped his hands together. "I'll give you a boost up."

She placed her hand as high up on the wagon as she could. Then she put her foot in his hands and he pushed her up. It was enough for her to make it to the seat.

"Oh, my!" she said breathlessly.

Dixon joined her on the seat. Joshua and Perry mounted the horses. Then Dixon called, "Pull out."

The mules moved forward causing the wagon to pitch before it settled into a smooth motion.

"Cap seems pretty taken with you."

Grace fanned her face, suddenly warm.

"Haven't seen him like this in years."

"You call him Cap?"

"Short for Captain. We used to work together in the cavalry."

"So, you've known him a long time then?"

Dixon nodded.

"And his daughter?"

Dixon sighed. "Victoria is lucky to have him as a father. Hate to think what her life would have been like without him."

Grace considered his words. From what Joshua told her, when Rachel died, Victoria was just a little girl. She would have no parent and no home. She would have died on her own. Or been taken by the Apache. Or worse.

"Something you need to know about Cap. He's brave and courageous and fiercely loyal. Almost to a fault. Most people never see his heart. All you have to do is see him with his daughter to know that he has a deep well of love to give."

Dixon rubbed one hand over his beard. "His heart is

fragile underneath it all. He is taken with you. It's written all over his face, so tread carefully, Miss Talbert."

They rode in silence for several miles. They started up the switchbacks and she watched for Joshua on the horse several yards in front of them. She saw Joshua's heart even if it was a small glimpse when he recounted the story about Rachel and Victoria. He hurt. Perhaps he loved Rachel and she did not return his love and that's what Dixon was trying to tell her.

She sighed wondering what would become of their relationship that started down in the valley. It was tenuous. She wanted to see him again to determine if their attraction was real and could develop into something more.

Certainly, he had experienced far more of life than she had. Years in the Army. Years developing his business and raising his daughter.

Grace was only twenty-two. She spent most of her life in San Francisco and only the last few years in Prescott. She remembered very little of London. Just that it rained all the time. She had seen and experienced so little of the world.

That was not entirely true. She knew firsthand how the Yuman-Apache were treated. Winter would be here soon enough and so many of the children were not clothed properly. The government refused to feed them, and she was determined to help.

She knew about the brothels on the street behind the saloons. She even knew that her father owned several, though she was not supposed to know. Three years ago, she overheard a conversation between some men and her father. Otherwise, she would be ignorant. Since that day, she tried to find a way to help those women. She enlisted Ira's help more than once to see that a crate of clothing and food accidentally fell off the wagon in front of the cribs. Grace's heart tightened. If she could rescue even one woman, she would.

Maybe she understood more of the world than she credited herself.

"How old is he?" she asked.

"Thirty-five last May."

Daddy would not be happy with a thirteen-year age gap. Truthfully, Daddy would be disappointed if she chose someone who did not benefit him.

CHAPTER 15

The sight of Prescott nestled in the valley below brought Joshua a sense of peace. They survived one night in the grasslands. He was glad they arrived close to when he promised Victoria that he would be home.

When they pulled in behind the freight office, he dismounted the horse. His abdomen, legs, and rear were sore. He was exhausted. Riding bareback took a great deal more effort than riding in a saddle. Thankfully his horse did not balk at it. Some horses would have.

Perry dismounted and took the reins of both horses to care for them.

Joshua helped Grace down from the freight wagon. She looked weary. Her hair was still down, and she looked beautiful albeit a little frazzled.

"Would you like me to get a carriage ready? Or I could walk you home?" he asked her.

"I can walk myself home. I'm sure you are eager to be reunited with your daughter."

He placed his hand on the small of her back and led her to the street.

"Yes, I am eager to see her. However, I would feel better knowing you made it home safely."

He dropped his hand to his side as she walked next to him.

"You'll see the crates are delivered to Camp Date Creek?" she asked.

He smiled. She was persistent. "Yes. My men will deliver them early in the week."

She turned her head toward him and caught his gaze.

"I promise."

Several minutes of silence ticked by. He wanted to say something, needed to say something. He just did not know what to say. His mind warred within him. Should he ask to see her again or should he wait to see if his feelings remained as strong?

He sighed. The only thing he knew for certain was that he did not want to get hurt again by falling for a woman who would never return his love. Twice was more than enough.

"This is my street," Grace said. "Third house down on the left."

Joshua reached for her arm and stopped her. He turned her to face him. His pulse rushed. She looked up at him with her tired gray-blue eyes.

"I…"

He was going to say he loved her. Silly. He did not know her.

Grace sighed. "Joshua, I'm exhausted. I know the last two days have been amazing and unusual and unexpected all at the same time. I am not looking for any grand declarations. I have no expectations."

A lump formed in his throat as he waited for the rejection.

"I don't know what that was. I do know I am interested in you. I believe you feel it too."

Not rejection. He nodded and cupped her face in his hand.

"Right now, I hope two things. First, that I might see you and Victoria at church tomorrow."

"Absolutely." He rubbed his thumb on her cheek.

"Second, that you will think on the past few days and if you still feel the same, I would be open to seeing you again." She let out a rushed breath.

For the first time in years, he allowed his heart to hope.

He placed his hands on her waist and whispered, "May I kiss you?"

She smiled, but her eyes flitted to her home. "I think it is better if you do not."

His shoulders tensed and he dropped his hands to his side.

"As you can see, I have arrived home safely." Grace reached up and kissed his cheek. "I look forward to seeing you and Victoria tomorrow."

She turned and started walking toward her house. She stopped and looked over her shoulder for a few seconds. Then she disappeared behind the large red door.

Joshua turned and headed towards his own home. She did not reject him. Nor did she fully accept him. Instead, she left them in limbo. She would be amenable to seeing him again.

It was so frustrating. What Grace said was wise. They had been fascinated with each other in a time of distress. Neither one of them should trust those feelings.

Blast it all. He was terrible with women. He gave his heart away too freely and too quickly. Maybe one day he would learn.

As he neared his house, he heard Victoria playing outside so he entered the gate on the side yard and joined her.

"Papa!"

The joy on her face filled his heart. He crouched down

and held his arms open wide. She ran to him and clutched his neck with all her might.

"I missed you, Pumpkin."

"I missed you, Papa. I hoped you would come back yesterday, but Miss Bethie told me you promised by tonight and that we should pray for God to keep you safe."

He squeezed her one last time before he released her and stood. He turned in a circle.

"As you can see, He did just that. Can you give me a minute with Miss Bethie?"

She nodded and danced around the yard.

"Sorry I didn't make it back last night. The wagon broke and we had to wait for help."

"We managed just fine, Mr. Harrison."

"Good."

Miss Bethie agreed to start supper later than normal so he could bathe beforehand.

Joshua plodded upstairs to his room. He grabbed a change of clothes and headed to the washroom. The water from the faucet was lukewarm. That was fine. He'd rather not lug heated water up the stairs.

He stripped down and eased himself into the claw-foot tub. He lathered up the soap and scrubbed everywhere.

Feelings churned inside of him. He wanted to be loved by a woman. He was thirty-five. He should have a wife and several children by now, more than his one adopted daughter.

He slid down into the tub and wet his hair. Then he scrubbed it with soap until the dirt washed away.

Guess starting over in a new town did not cure his loneliness. He swallowed hard. He wanted a wife so much his stomach ached. Love just never seemed to work out in his favor.

These last two days with Grace hit him hard. She was beautiful, idealistic, graceful, and kind. She knew exactly how to help him when his panic threatened to pull him under. Her smile was inviting. Everything about her seemed to fill that emptiness in him. And not in half measure, but in full measure.

As Joshua dried off and dressed, he could not shake off the self-recrimination. He pushed too hard. He scared her away. He was dangerously close to failing at love again.

He joined Miss Bethie and Victoria for supper listening as his daughter shared everything that happened while he was gone. His mind still chewed on his failure and regret the rest of the evening until he fell into a fitful sleep.

CHAPTER 16

"Miss Grace," Kingsley greeted her as she entered her home. "Mr. Talbert has been very worried about you."

"Grace! Is that you?"

She took a deep breath as Daddy hurried to the entry-way.

"Are you alright? What happened?" He grabbed her arms and looked her over.

She leaned in gave him a kiss on the cheek before pulling away.

"I'm fine, Daddy. Just exhausted."

He frowned. "We need to talk."

Grace sighed and her shoulders sagged. "Can I clean up and meet you in the parlor in an hour?"

Daddy pursed his lips. That was not good. He was angry about something.

"Go," he said tersely.

"Kingsley, please ask Mercy to draw me a bath."

"Yes, Miss Grace. Good to have you home."

Grace climbed the stairs slowly nervous about what caused Daddy to be in a state. She entered her room. She saw her reflection in the mirror. She looked ghastly! Dirt streaked her face. Her hair was a tangled matted mess.

Mercy knocked on the door before entering. She went into Grace's private washroom and ran a bath. While the tub filled, she came back into Grace's room.

"Do you want me to brush your hair out?" Mercy asked.

Grace nodded and took a seat in front of her vanity.

Mercy started at the ends and brushed for several minutes. She went into the washroom and turned off the water. Then she came back and brushed some more.

"We were caught in a monsoon storm," Grace explained.

"I think that is the best I can do, Miss Grace. Do you need anything else?"

Grace dismissed her.

She stripped down and went into the washroom. The bath water steamed, and she hopped in. She slid down to wet her hair. When her hair was damp, she grabbed the special egg-based hair cleanser that Mercy mixed up for her. She rubbed it into her long locks and on her scalp, massaging it throughout. Then she rinsed her hair with a vinegar and lilac solution.

Her heart fluttered. Joshua asked to kiss her. It was tempting to allow him to do so. She would have enjoyed it.

Thankfully her mind won that battle. It was wise to take some space and time to sort out her feelings. She barely knew him. He hardly knew her. She did not want a relationship built on enthralling attraction that faded too quickly. She wanted a man of character. A man of integrity. Determining if Joshua was those things would take time. She hoped he was.

Grace finished her bath and dressed in her pale green house dress. Simple. Comfortable. Stylish enough if any guests came by, she would be presentable.

She joined her father in the parlor and dried her hair by the fire.

"What did you want to speak to me about?" she asked

her father.

"Are you alright? Did that man… Did he take advantage of you?"

She snorted. "I find it incredibly ironic that you should be so concerned for my virtue."

Her father frowned. "What is that supposed to mean?"

She sat on the chair closest to the fireplace, smoothing out her damp hair. "For someone who owns several brothels, I did not figure a woman's virtue was important to you."

"Grace." His eyes smoldered and the edge in his tone warned her to stop.

"My virtue is intact. Josh… Mr. Harrison is a respectable man and treated me appropriately. I just find it unbelievable that you can live with your double standard."

Her father stood. "Do not speak to me that way. Your mother was right. I spoil you."

"So, this is my fault?" Grace raised her voice. "You've spoiled me so when I challenge the inconsistencies of your character you turn it on me?"

Her father closed his eyes and took several breaths. When he spoke again, his voice was calm and soft. "I was merely making sure you were not harmed. I love you, sweetheart."

Her righteous indignation took over. "As you can see, I am fine. What makes you think that Mr. Harrison would do anything to compromise me?"

"You are naive. The suitors that have come and gone over the years have been vetted by me. He was not."

And that was the real issue.

"Make no mistake, I know exactly who Mr. Harrison is. I know everything about him, and he is far too old for you. He's thirty-five and never been married. I caution you, Grace, such a man is worldly."

Grace bit her lower lip. She despised when her father danced around a subject with veiled words. He never came out and said what he meant. He strongly implied that Joshua could not be trusted because he assumed that Joshua dallied with women since he had never been married. That was ludicrous.

"Just how much digging did you do, Father?" He was Daddy when they were on good terms and Father when they were not.

"When a wealthy businessman enters my town and stares at my daughter during a funeral, I make it my business to know everything about him. Every skeleton in his closet and every hidden secret."

Grace lifted her chin. Father did not like Joshua that much was clear.

"He is no good for you. Stop this foolish infatuation and pursue someone closer to your age."

"Someone more like Alex? Did you forget that he was nine years my senior?"

"Yes, but he has an impeccable character."

"And political ambitions. You believe if I marry him, he will be manipulated by you. But he won't. Alex has more integrity than that."

Father sighed and sank onto the settee. "I do not want to argue with you. I'm glad you are home and safe."

Grace swallowed back the rest of her opinions. She did not trust that Father had her best interests in mind. Clearly, he believed he could gain nothing if she associated with Joshua. She tapped her foot in a staccato rhythm. Sometimes she wished she had a normal father. One with no hidden agenda or unquenchable ambition.

Kingsley announced that supper was served. She stood and tossed her damp locks over her shoulder. She lifted her chin, straightened her back, and marched upstairs to her room.

"Have Mercy bring up a tray!" she shouted down the stairwell. Let Father dine alone.

CHAPTER 17

Joshua entered the quaint church building with his daughter Victoria. He spotted Grace walking toward the front. She took a seat alone.

"This is the second week in a row that Alex Glassman has not escorted Miss Talbert to church," a woman whispered to her friend behind him.

"Look," the second woman said. "He is sitting in his sister's pew."

Until that moment, Joshua never considered that Grace could be spoken for. His heart twisted.

"Papa, can we sit over there near my friend from school?"

"Sure thing, Pumpkin."

He followed her to the end of the pew and away from the gossips. When he stepped into the aisle, a young boy darted in front of him.

"Boone Colter! Get over here."

Joshua turned to see a face from his past. She recognized him instantly.

"Lieutenant. I mean Captain." Hannah Colter gave him a big hug.

"Just Joshua now," he said swallowing the hard lump in his throat.

Will Colter came up next to his wife and put an arm

around her. His greeting was significantly colder. "Harrison."

"How have you been?" Hannah asked brightly. Her eyes wandered to the front of the room. "Boone!"

A red-headed boy skidded to a stop next to her. She placed a firm hand on his shoulder.

"I'm so sorry. How have you been Joshua?"

"Well."

"Papa," Victoria murmured under her breath. "Who is this?"

"Hannah, Will, this is my daughter, Victoria."

"Oh, my!" Hannah exclaimed. Her brows drew together for a brief moment before a smile lit her face. "It's a pleasure to meet you."

"Boys!" Hannah called. "Come meet my old friend."

Five boys lined up next to her. She placed a hand on each one's head as she introduced them. "This is James. Samuel. Boone, my rowdy one. Deacon. And Preston is the youngest." She pointed to the toddler in Will's arms.

Joshua's palms grew sweaty. Clearly, they wasted no time starting a family. Five boys in the last eight years.

"Papa. My friend," Victoria whispered tugging on his arm.

"It was nice to see you, Hannah. Will."

Joshua followed his daughter to the next pew and sat in front of the large Colter family. At least he wouldn't have to look at them the whole service.

"When did he get back?" he heard Will ask.

"I don't know," Hannah replied. "His daughter is older than I expected."

Joshua smiled. He didn't mind that Hannah did the math and it did not add up. She made her choice and from all appearances was satisfied with it.

The music started and his gaze traveled to where Grace stood alone. She wore a rust-colored dress with black lace around the neckline which revealed much more of her ivory skin than the brown high collared dress she wore the other day. When she looked his way, she smiled, and his face warmed.

The music stopped. Victoria yanked his hand. "Sit down."

He quickly sat once he realized he was the only one still standing.

The pastor gave a stirring message, but Joshua was too distracted to pay close attention. His eyes kept straying to Grace.

If he could believe the gossips earlier, it sounded like she had a beau as recently as two weeks ago. She said nothing down in the grasslands. She kissed him back and welcomed his touch. Those were not the actions of a woman pining over another man.

The pastor dismissed the service. Joshua stood and led Victoria out of the church.

"Papa, can we stay for the potluck?"

"Uh… We didn't bring anything to share, Pumpkin."

"That's alright," Grace said next to him. "There will be plenty."

He turned and smiled at Grace. Her face lit with a grin and her gray-blue eyes reflected the light. That dress looked stunning on her.

He cleared his throat. "Are you staying?"

"Of course."

Victoria hurried away with her friend.

"It looks like we are staying," he said. His eyes held her gaze. The sun warmed his back as her smile warmed his soul. He wanted to say he missed her. He wanted to whisk her away to a private corner and talk with her. Tell her how miserable he was without her.

"James! Boone!" Hannah Colter's voice echoed across the church yard. The oldest boy pushed his way between Grace and Joshua right as his mother caught up to him. "Take your brother and go stand in line with your father."

"Mama!" her oldest whined.

She glowered at him, and he scurried away.

Grace spoke up. "Joshua, this is Hannah Colter."

"Oh, we're old friends," Hannah said. "My first husband and I met Joshua on our wagon train to the Arizona Territory."

She turned toward him. "How long have you been back?"

"Two weeks."

"Oh. I wish you would have let us know you were coming. We would have had you out for supper."

Joshua glanced over to where Will stood in line. Will frowned and Joshua doubted that he would be invited to their ranch ever.

Grace excused herself. He started to reach for her hand, but she was gone.

Hannah asked him several questions and shared some news of her family until Will brought her a plate and stole her away.

Joshua let out a slow breath. The feelings he once thought he had for Hannah were buried a long time ago. She chose Will Colter. Joshua was then assigned to the First Cavalry at Fort Goodwin and out of their lives. It must have been a shock to see him at their church. He appreciated that Hannah tried to make him feel welcome, but he would steer clear of her the rest of the day.

He scanned the crowd and spotted Victoria with her

friend. Miss Bethie hovered nearby, so he walked to the back of the food line.

———

Grace walked around and greeted several of her friends from the Women's Aid Society while keeping one eye on the conversation between Hannah Colter and Joshua. They were old friends. Her heart squeezed.

When she first spotted Hannah speaking with him before service, she thought it was odd. The way he looked at Hannah, there had been something there once.

She spotted Joshua moving to the back of the line and she hurried to catch up with him.

"Mind if I join you?" she asked as her heart pounded.

He smiled and placed his hand on the small of her back to guide her in front of him. Waves of warmth spread from his touch.

She took a plate and dished up food as they walked through the line.

"How do you know Hannah?" she asked.

Joshua fumbled with the serving spoon almost dropping it. He sighed. "I was friends with her first husband."

Grace gasped. "What do you mean her first husband? Isn't that Will?"

"His name was Drew. Drew Anderson. I was assigned to escort the first territorial governor's wagon train from Kansas to Arizona. She and Drew were on the wagon train."

Joshua plopped a big spoonful of mashed potatoes onto his plate.

"He died in the mountains north of here, so I helped drive her wagon the rest of the way."

Grace frowned. She had no idea Hannah had ever been

married to anyone other than Will Colter. Or that she had been widowed.

She glanced over at him as he finished dishing up his food. His shoulders drooped. When he realized she was watching him, his demeanor changed. He straightened his back and smiled.

"Let's sit over here in the shade."

He set his plate on the ground and helped her down. Then he crossed his legs and leaned back against the tree trunk. It reminded her of their time in the grasslands. It felt like years ago. Yet, it had been only two days.

She studied him as he ate. There was a sadness lingering in his eyes.

"You not hungry?" he teased her.

She laughed it off and took a bite of her food.

"Did you love her?"

Joshua's hand froze midway from his plate to his mouth. He set the fork back on the plate.

"I thought I did."

"What happened?" she asked as her ribs squeezed the air from her lungs.

"It was a long time ago." He took another bite of food.

She searched his eyes. He looked away. He did love her. Not presently, but at one time he had.

Joshua flashed her a bright smile. "I heard an interesting rumor before church?"

She forced a smile at his change of topic. "Mr. Harrison, I would not have thought you a busybody."

He stuffed some food in his mouth. When he swallowed, he pointed his fork at her. "Normally, I'm not. But this rumor caught my attention. It seems that a particular young woman who fervently kissed me on the grasslands in the rain was recently seen without her beau for the last two weeks."

His smile faded and his lips formed a thin line as he looked directly at her, piercing her with his gaze. His eyes narrowed.

Grace swallowed as heat warmed her face. She fidgeted with the lace edging of her sleeve. Her breath shallowed. "I suppose you are talking about Alex."

He raised an eyebrow. "I believe his name is Alex Glassman, yes."

"Alex Glassman was a suitor handpicked by my father. He is the ideal son-in-law for my father—smart, wealthy, and politically ambitious."

Joshua frowned. "And you don't like smart, wealthy, ambitious men."

"Politically ambitious," she said.

"I stand corrected."

She sighed. "I do not love Alex. And he does not love me. He loves the idea of me or of a wife, I should say. He did hope to garner my father's support. But he dislikes my ideals and does not love me."

"And he broke off the courtship?" Joshua asked still holding her gaze.

Grace sat up straighter and lifted her chin. She narrowed her eyes. "Actually, I was the one who broke it off, if you must know."

When he looked away, she took another bite of food before setting her plate aside.

"Do you think it is wise to be seen sitting with another man under the shade of a tree so shortly after the end of your relationship?"

"Honestly, Joshua, I don't know what you want from me."

He set his plate aside.

"Did I mean anything to you?" he asked, the hurt dripped from his tone.

"Do you think I go around flinging myself into just any man's arms? That kiss was real. The feelings you stir in me are real. I have never experienced anything like it before. Not with Alex. Not with any suitor." Her hands shook at her raw confession.

He reached for her hand. "I'm sorry."

Grace pulled her hand away. "Were you toying with me?"

"No. I… It was real for me too."

"Then why are you being so utterly hurtful right now?" She stood as the tears started to fall. She had to get away.

"Grace!" he called after her.

She hurried from the church yard and down the street toward home.

It's not like she had known him even a week yet. What did he expect? That she should sit at home like some nun waiting to court until he dropped into her life. She had not misled him. She had not done anything wrong.

Grace slowed her steps and stopped in the town park and sat down on a bench. She expected nothing from him. She understood he lived a life long before her. The relationship, or whatever it was, with Hannah Colter was a shock. She felt the jealousy rise. But she knew that was an unrealistic expectation.

Her eyes blurred. She retrieved her handkerchief and dried them. Then she squared her shoulders and strode the rest of the way home vowing to avoid Joshua Harrison from that point forward.

CHAPTER 18

Joshua kicked himself. What an idiot he was. He wanted to run after Grace, but he could not leave Victoria.

He stayed under the shade of the cottonwood tree and finished his lunch. Then he delivered his plate and hers to the washing area.

"Who was that man Miss Talbert was with?" A nearby busybody asked her friend. "Wasn't she just with Alex Glassman?"

Joshua scuffed away from the conversation, emotions churning. Seeing Hannah threw him more than he thought it would. Probably because she looked so happy, and she had everything he longed for. She had someone to love who loved her back. She had a family, quite a large family.

Then to find out Grace had been in a relationship with someone else. Two weeks was barely enough time to be over a lost love. But she did say that she did not love Glassman and he did not love her. Perhaps the relationship never even bloomed.

How was he going to fix this?

"Papa!" Victoria pranced over to his side. "Can I go over to Lottie's house for the afternoon? Miss Bethie said she would walk me home in a few hours."

"Did Lottie's mama say it's alright?"

"Yes."

He gave her a hug and kissed the top of her head. "See you later, Pumpkin."

Victoria flitted away with her friend from school.

Joshua sighed and headed back home. He sat in the front parlor and tried to read a book. After reading the same paragraph three times, he closed the book.

Grace had asked if he toyed with her. Had he? He knew very little about her before they went on that trip and were stranded. His attraction to her was stronger than any other woman in his past. Even more than Victoria's mother.

Kissing her had been impulsive. If he was honest with himself, it was the way she looked at him that drove him to it. It was the first time a woman looked at him with anticipation. It made him feel wanted.

He needed to stop licking his wounds over past relationships if he wanted a chance for something real with Grace. Wallowing in self-pity and envy was getting him nowhere.

He needed to apologize. He needed to make things right with her.

———

Grace's heart felt no better by midweek. No matter, she had an organization to run. She chose an emerald green dress and black hat with a large emerald green feather. She fixed her hair, checked her appearance, and left her home.

Dark ominous clouds hung low in the sky. She forgot an umbrella, so if it did rain, she would have to wait it out at the Women's Aid Society's building.

She arrived at a quarter till nine with plenty of time to set up for their meeting at half past. She retrieved the pitchers and a tray from the kitchen and went out back to fill them with water. She propped the door open and maneuvered the tray with the pitchers through the doorway.

On each table, she placed a doily in the center. Then she set a pitcher and several glasses on each one. She arranged the dessert plates and silverware on the table next to a stack of napkins.

A knock sounded at the door. She glanced at the clock. Nine. The ladies would not arrive for twenty minutes or more.

"Grace," Joshua greeted her when she opened the door.

For a few seconds she thought about closing it again. Instead, she stepped aside and let him enter.

"I wanted to apologize—"

"We have a meeting this morning and the ladies will be here soon. Now is not a good time."

He reached for her hand. She dodged him.

His shoulders fell. "I wanted to let you know all the crates were fine. Dixon delivered them on Monday. He said to tell you the," he cleared his throat, "Indians appreciated the goods."

She tapped her foot on the floor.

"Is there anything else?"

"When can we talk?" His voice was soft. "Grace, I need to talk to you. Please."

"Come back at noon. You can escort me home."

When he did not move, she motioned to the door. He left and she closed the door behind him.

The ladies arrived for their large planning meeting. She was so distracted that Martha Stanton asked her the same question three times before Grace responded. The usual joy she felt leading the meeting had vanished the moment Joshua showed up that morning.

"Is everything alright?" Rebecca Quinn asked in her lovely southern accent. Grace loved listening to her talk.

"I'm fine."

"I saw you at church with Mr. Harrison. It seemed like he upset you."

Heat warmed the apples of her cheeks. "I don't want to talk about it."

"If you change your mind, you are welcome to stop by for tea later."

Grace thanked her. Several women stayed to help clean up, so they finished with twenty minutes to spare.

She paced back and forth as she waited for Joshua to return. She was tempted to walk home without speaking to him, but her heart would not let her. She still cared for him.

Joshua arrived promptly at noon. "Can I take you to lunch? There is a new café down the street."

Grace agreed and locked up the building before taking his arm.

"I'm sorry for being so antagonistic at church. I had not expected to see Hannah and was not prepared for the old wounds it opened. I ended up taking it out on you and for that I am very sorry."

She sighed. "I understand."

He placed her hand in the crook of his arm. "I was also caught off guard when I heard you had been in a relationship. I was mad at myself for not asking you before I kissed you."

They arrived at the café and were seated near a window. Once they ordered Joshua picked up the conversation again.

"You said that Alex was someone your father wanted for a son-in-law and that all your suitors had been handpicked. What do you want?"

I want you. She sighed. "My mama's parting words were 'Marry for love.' She must have seen that my heart's desire was just that. She knew that Daddy has a way of getting what he wants. I think what she was trying to tell me was not to let Daddy manipulate or bully me into marrying someone for his benefit."

"Would he really do that?"

"I don't know. I have never crossed him before. But I am past the age of consent and can decide for myself." She looked down at her hands.

Joshua reached across the table and took one in his hands. "What is it?"

"With Mama gone, I'm all the family Daddy has left. I would hate to marry someone he does not approve of. Yet, I'm not sure he will ever approve of someone I choose."

The food arrived so he let go of her hand. He said a blessing over the meal, and they continued.

"Would you ever choose someone that Victoria did not like?" she asked.

He frowned. "I don't think I would ever choose someone she didn't. If that were the case, then I would have chosen poorly."

Grace picked at the food on her plate. Her fight with Daddy weighed on her mind. He made it very clear he did not approve of Joshua. Since he was the only man her heart chose, she could be in for trouble with her father.

"Daddy said he knew every skeleton in your closet."

Joshua laughed. "I'd love to know what skeletons I have. I've already told you about Hannah and Rachel and Victoria. Everything else is life happening. I have nothing to hide."

"I don't mean to sound disparaging, but Daddy tends not to let things go. If he does not approve of this relationship, he could make trouble for you."

He grinned from ear to ear. "This relationship?"

Heat warmed her cheeks.

"Are you asking me to court you?"

"What if I were?" she asked, coyly.

Joshua cleared his throat. "Grace Talbert, may I have your permission to court you?"

She smiled as her heart picked up pace. "Yes, Mr. Harrison, please do court me."

They finished the meal and headed out the door. Thunder sounded overhead and the skies dumped an onslaught of rain. Joshua grabbed her hand as they ran down the boardwalk to his office.

She laughed as they entered the building. "I hope it doesn't rain every time we're together."

Joshua's eyes sparkled with laughter. "If so, we might be responsible for turning the desert into a rain forest."

He took her hands and pulled her to him. Grace's breath shallowed as he put his arms around her. "Might there be kissing in this courtship?"

"I have no doubts."

Then he lowered his head and captured her lips in a sweet, but restrained kiss. She returned the kiss as warmth flooded her from head to toe. When he stopped the kiss, she rested her head against his chest.

"I could hold you forever, Grace."

"I could let you."

He cleared his throat. "I should ask your father for permission. It's the right thing to do."

"I don't think he will give it. Besides, I am past the age of consent and can choose for myself."

He released his arms from her and looked down into her eyes. "Are you sure? I can speak to him soon."

"Would you walk away from me if he says no?"

His gaze shifted to the window. His voice was soft when he spoke. "No, I don't think I could."

"Then it is settled," she said.

Seeing that the rain let up to a light sprinkle, she added, "I really should be going."

"Let me walk you home."

She kissed him on the cheek. She needed to delay Daddy finding out just a little longer. "I'll be fine. See you soon?"

He nodded as she left.

CHAPTER 19

"Papa! Papa!"

Victoria's screams pulled Joshua from his sleep early Saturday morning. He pulled on a pair of pants and ran into her room.

"Papa!" she sobbed uncontrollably.

"What is it, Pumpkin?"

Light came in through the window. He looked around and then he saw it. Blood.

His heart stopped. She was hurt.

"Are you hurt?"

"Am I dying? Papa, there's blood!"

He knew he saw it. His heart raced. Think. Think.

"Miss Bethie!"

Victoria sobbed. "She's not here."

Darn it. She was visiting her family's ranch for a few days.

Every muscle in his body tightened. "Let me fetch the doctor. You stay here. Be brave for me. I'll be back just as soon as I can."

Joshua kissed the top of her head and gave her a hug before he ran back to his room and put on his shoes. He grabbed a shirt and put it on as he flew down the stairs and out the front door. The doctor's office was several blocks away, but he ran the whole way.

When he arrived, the door was locked! He pounded on the door but there was no answer. Then he noticed the sign in the window. "Out at Henderson farm."

Joshua cursed. He ran his hands through his hair. He started to turn back towards home. Then he turned the other way.

Grace. Grace could help him.

He ran down the street. It was just after dawn. He hoped she was up already. Victoria needed him.

He kept on running until he made it to Grace's house. He beat the door with a fist as he gasped for air.

"Grace—"

"Sir?" A man in a suit answered the door.

"Is. Grace." He gasped for more air. "Home?"

"Miss Talbert is—"

"Kingsley, I say, what is all the commotion?" A man's voice asked.

Joshua pushed his way into the house.

"Grace!"

She came into the entryway. "Joshua, what is it?"

"Victoria. Need help." Another gulp of air. "Doctor at farm."

Fear widened her eyes. "What happened?"

"There's blood!"

Grace took a deep breath. "Let's go."

"Grace, what is going on?" The man asked as she ushered Joshua out the door.

"I'll send word if I'll be gone long," she said over her shoulder.

"We have to hurry!" Joshua grabbed her hand and led her through the town at a brisk pace.

"Joshua, you're scaring me. What happened?"

"I... I don't know. She woke up screaming. There was

blood."

Grace stopped.

"What are you doing? We have to go!"

"Joshua," she said very calmly. "How old is Victoria?"

"Eleven."

Still, she would not move. He grabbed her hand and tugged.

"Joshua. She'll be fine."

"How can you say that?"

She sighed and picked up the pace again. "Because I think I know what is wrong."

His throat tightened. "What? Tell me!"

"How to put this delicately? She is at an age when many young girls start the process of becoming a woman."

Joshua stopped. Heat warmed his face. He didn't know. He knew, but he never thought about that. He never talked to... Ugh!

They walked at a normal pace the rest of the way home. He was a total failure as a father. Grace was probably right. And he had done nothing to prepare Victoria for that moment.

He opened the door and led Grace upstairs. Victoria still cried.

When he tried to follow Grace into the room, she stopped him.

"Relax. I will explain to her everything and what to expect. Would you go make us some coffee?"

"But I should—"

"She is not going to want to talk to her papa about this."

He hovered outside the door leaning against the wall.

"Victoria? I'm Miss Grace. We met at church. Do you remember me?"

Victoria hiccupped. "Yes."

"You are going to be just fine. When a young girl reaches a certain age, her body changes. This is part of becoming a woman. God designed us this way."

Joshua plodded down the stairs with heavy footfalls. Grace was right, Victoria would not want to talk to him about that. He wasn't sure he wanted to hear Grace explain it all either.

He started the stove and set a pot of water on to boil then he sank into a chair. He propped his elbows on the table and dropped his head into his hands as the adrenaline left his body. It's not like he was clueless about that topic. He just never even thought about it or how it might be important to explain it to his daughter *before* it happened to her.

Grace came down the stairs sometime later and finished making the coffee. She poured him a cup and stood beside him. She rubbed a hand on his back.

"How is she?"

"She's fine. She's washing up and getting dressed for the day. After breakfast, I'll show her how to clean the sheets."

"I'm a terrible father," he moaned.

"Joshua, you could not have known. Women have gone through this since the beginning of creation. She will be fine, albeit a little embarrassed today."

He leaned back and sipped the coffee.

"Would you like some breakfast?" she asked.

"I can do that."

She let out a sigh of relief. "Good. I'm not the best cook."

He smiled. "And you would have let us suffer through it?"

"I can make eggs. And I can make eggs."

He laughed. "So, what you're saying is you can make

only eggs?"

"Yes. And they aren't that great. I guess that's just how it is when you grow up in household with a cook."

Joshua whipped up a batch of pancakes and some bacon. He held up two eggs. "Should I observe your technique?"

Grace laughed. "No. I'll watch you from here. Make sure you're doing it right."

He cracked the eggs and fried them. "Sunny side up or over easy?"

"Over easy."

Victoria came down and joined them in the kitchen. She sat in a chair but wouldn't look at him. Joshua set a plate in front of Grace and one for Victoria. Then he sat down with his plate. He held out his hands and each of his girls took one. When he finished praying, he released their hands.

"Dig in, Pumpkin."

Victoria looked at him and he winked. She smiled and poured syrup on her pancakes.

"Oh, this is good," Grace said pointing to the pancakes. "Yours rival Esther's."

He laughed and mouthed the words, "Thank you."

The banter continued throughout breakfast, and he couldn't help but wonder if that was what it would be like to be married to Grace. He could get used to that.

Joshua stood and placed their dishes in the wash basin while he waited for the water to heat.

"You may want to straighten your buttons," Grace teased as she took Victoria to the laundry room to clean the sheets.

He looked down at his shirt. Sure enough, he skipped a few buttons and the ones that were fastened were misaligned. He sighed and fixed his shirt. When the water finished heating, he poured it into the wash basin and washed the dishes. Then he poured another cup of coffee and sat at the table.

Grace and Victoria came back into the kitchen. He nodded to the coffee pot and raised an eyebrow. Grace nodded. As she sat at the table, he placed the coffee mug in front of her.

"Papa, can I go read my book?"

"Yes, Pumpkin."

When Victoria left, Joshua said, "I suppose the man in your entryway was your father."

She nodded.

He sighed. "Some first impression I made, huh?"

She smiled. "I'll smooth it over with him when I get back home."

"I'm sorry. I really should have realized what was going on."

Reaching for his hand, she took it and squeezed. "It's alright. I was happy to help and to meet your daughter. She really is a very sweet girl."

"Thank you. I try my best. I just don't always know what to do."

Grace laughed. "Does anyone? As my friends have married and had children, I have always marveled how no two are alike. We think that we will instinctively know the best way to raise children, but life throws unexpected things at us. A child with a strong will. Another is sensitive and quiet. Another is always risking things and getting into trouble. Seems to me like parenthood is one long experience full of joys and sorrows, triumphs and trials."

When she spoke like that, it was easy to forget how young she was, for she was absolutely right.

She finished her coffee and stood. "I should head home. Daddy will be worried by now."

He stood and stepped closer. He took her hands in his. "Thank you for rescuing me today."

She hugged him close and gave him a kiss on the cheek. "See you at church tomorrow?"

He nodded and escorted her to the front door.

———

Grace smiled as she stepped down onto the sidewalk. The sun warmed her back as she started toward home. She was honored to help Joshua and Victoria through a difficult morning.

She imagined Victoria would never forget the morning, even though she calmed down considerably after Grace explained everything. Poor sweet girl. It had to be a shock.

She felt sorry for Joshua too. Raising a daughter by himself was no small task. Though he had a housekeeper to help, she knew it was not the same as if he had a wife.

Her heart raced at the thought. They were courting. Things were going well. Perhaps her courtship with Joshua would lead to marriage. If so, she needed to be prepared, not only to be his wife, but to be a mother to his daughter.

A wagon sped by kicking up a cloud of dust. Grace slowed her steps. She was not sure she was ready to be a wife or a mother.

She loved her work with the Women's Aid Society. Would she be able continue her charitable efforts? Would he demand she stop like Alex had?

What she did with the Women's Aid Society fulfilled her. She was made to help others. She was organized and efficient. If she had to step down, who would take over? Did she even want to?

She sighed and scolded herself for borrowing trouble

from tomorrow. They just started courting. She did not have to work out all such details right then. She needed to focus on getting to know Joshua and Victoria. Let the relationship take a natural course. Perhaps none of her worries were even founded.

Picking up her pace, she resolved to leave her worries behind. Time was on her side. If changes were needed, she would figure it out when the time came.

CHAPTER 20

A week later, Joshua headed over to Grace's house. Miss Bethie watched Victoria so he and Grace could enjoy an afternoon outing. He pulled the carriage to a stop in front of her house. When he knocked on the door, Kingsley greeted him.

"Afternoon, sir."

"Is Grace ready?"

"One moment please," Kingsley said as he opened the door and showed Joshua to the parlor.

Joshua stood and looked around the ornately decorated room. A fireplace lined one wall. There were several groupings of chairs with side tables throughout the room. A chaise lounge sat near the fireplace.

"Mr. Harrison."

Joshua stiffened and turned around.

"I'm Grace's father, Simon Talbert."

Joshua extended his hand in greeting. When Simon took his hand, he squeezed hard and narrowed his eyes.

"You should break this off now," Simon warned before releasing Joshua's hand. "You are much too old for her."

Well, it looked like Grace assessed her father accurately. If he had asked him for permission, her father obviously would have said no. She wanted Joshua and he wanted her. So, he would fight for her if need be.

"She can make up her own mind."

"I'm warning you—"

"Yes, I understood that Mr. Talbert. I mean no disrespect, but Grace is old enough to choose for herself."

"Daddy!" Grace scolded as she entered the parlor. "Be nice. He may one day end up being your son-in-law." She laid a hand on her father's arm and directed him to a chair. She placed a kiss on his cheek. "I'll be back before sundown."

Then she turned her attention to Joshua. "I'm ready."

He offered his arm and escorted her out of the house without a farewell to Simon.

"I'm sorry," she said.

"You heard that."

"Enough of it to know Daddy doesn't like you."

He sighed. "He doesn't even know me."

Joshua helped her into the carriage. Then he got in and started the horses forward.

"He'll come around," she said. "But let's enjoy each other's company instead of talking about my dour father."

He smiled. "Agreed."

"Where are we going?"

"I found a nice spot near a creek in the woods. Great place for a picnic."

When they arrived, he helped her out of the carriage. Then he laid out a blanket and set the basket on the ground. He helped Grace sit down.

She breathed deeply and let out a long, satisfied breath. "It's lovely here."

He sat down next to her and pulled her close. Looking into her eyes, he said, "Yes, it's lovely here."

Then he lowered his lips to hers showing her how much he missed her these last few days. He deepened the kiss and she responded, looping her arms around his neck. He lowered her down to the ground and slowed the kiss. Then he leaned on one arm. Her breathing caused her chest to rise and fall. He traced a finger down her cheek to her neck.

A corner of his mouth curled up. He ran a finger along the edge of her dress across her soft skin. She held her breath. Then he lowered his lips to hers again, searching deeply and fervently. He kissed her neck as he relished her closeness.

"Joshua."

She placed a hand on his shoulder and pushed him away. Then she sat up. He followed her lead and sat up as well. She let out a shaky breath then smiled.

"Do you always have dessert before lunch?" she teased.

"Hmm. I could get used to that."

She slid further away from him and opened the basket. "I do hope there's no crust on my sandwich."

He winked at her.

She squealed in delight when she set out the sandwiches and not even one had crust. "Fancy sandwiches."

He laughed. "Miss Bethie thought I was crazy when I asked her to cut off the crust."

"How did you find this place?" she asked, taking a bite of her fancy sandwich.

"Thomas Anderson told me about it. Said he and his wife like to come here when they have someone to watch the kids. It's as quiet and peaceful as he said."

He ate his sandwich and studied her. "Would you break off our courtship if your father asked you to?"

She snorted. "He already did, so I think you have your answer."

Joshua frowned. "I don't mean to come between you."

"Daddy is used to getting his way. He doesn't quite

know what to do with me right now. But I know I'm not being foolish." She looked out toward the creek. "I do hope he comes around. I would like his blessing, but I won't demand it and I won't change my mind if he chooses not to give it."

His gut tightened. He knew how close she was to her father. He hoped she never had to choose between himself or him.

"I am headed down to Camp Date Creek on Thursday with Belinda and her husband."

Joshua's breath shallowed. "I don't think that's a good idea. Dixon just came back yesterday and said there over five hundred Indians there."

"That's why we're going. We've heard that many are sick with malaria and have no medical care. We have some supplies and can help ease their suffering."

"Grace, I don't want you to go."

"You need to understand, that whether I am single or one day married, I plan to help the poor and sick, whether they live on a reservation or in town. This is important to me."

Joshua's heart ached. "I don't think it's safe right now. Dixon said there was a lot of tension when he and Perry drove through. I just don't want to see you get hurt."

"I won't get hurt. I'll be helping. Belinda and her husband will be there. We'll be fine."

She reached for his hand and squeezed it. "I promise."

He looked away. He couldn't lose her. He had only just found her. It was useless to argue with her. She would go regardless.

"Tell me about Victoria's mother," she said.

Joshua coughed as the knife twisted in his chest. "Let's walk along the creek."

He stood and helped her to her feet. Then he led them to the bank of the creek. "Here you stand on this side away from the bank. I wouldn't want you falling in." He smiled.

"Why, thank you my knight in shining armor." She giggled.

They walked several paces while he tried to work up the courage to tell her the story. She intertwined her fingers with his.

"Everyone in my company out of Fort Goodwin knew the Widow Feagan. She lost her husband a few months before I arrived at the fort and began patrolling the area around the Gila River.

"After the attack and my capture, Dixon made his way back to the fort, but was in rough shape so he could not come looking for me. When," his voice cracked, "the Indians dumped me on Widow Feagan's doorstep, she took me in and nursed me back to health while caring for a three-year-old, and farming."

He took a deep breath. It was hard to talk about her even though it had been over seven years ago.

"Sounds like she had a very difficult life."

"She did. Two months after I arrived and while I was still recovering, Dixon found me. He reminded me that when I was on my feet again, I needed to return to the fort. I didn't want to. I had already fallen in love with Rachel and thought if I had more time with her, she would eventually…"

A tear trailed down his cheek. He cleared his throat as he wiped it away. It was too hard to admit out loud that she never loved him.

He closed his eyes and breathed deeply of the pine fragrance in the air. Birds chirped to each other. The creek gurgled along unaware of how it soothed his deep wounds.

"Victoria is the spitting image of her mother. The dark brown curls. Bright blue eyes. Cute freckles dusting her cheeks. I'm going to miss those freckles. They've already started fading.

"A month after his first visit, Dixon came back. I was in good health, and it was time to go, so I left with him.

"The next time we were out on patrol we noticed there was no smoke from Widow Feagan's chimney." It was easier to speak of her as a widow rather than say her name.

"I rode over. Dixon followed closely behind me. She was lying on the ground. Arrows…"

He coughed and pinched the bridge of his nose.

"She was covered in them. When we got to her, she wheezed. Victoria sat next to her crying, unharmed."

His breaths came in short bursts as he recalled the image in his mind. The horror. He had never seen such savagery before or since. Not in battles. Not in wars.

"Her dying words were, 'Take Victoria as your own.'"

A few more tears ran down his face. He turned to Grace. "I promised her I would."

Grace reached up and wiped his cheek with her thumb. Then she pulled him close for a hug.

Her compassion undid him. The years of hurt and anger gushed forth. He clung to her as if she was his only lifeline.

Several minutes passed before he regained his composure and stepped back.

"I took Victoria back to the fort with me. Then I mustered out of the Army. My commitment had ended earlier that year and I was at a point where I needed to decide to re-enlist or leave. I knew I could not care for her while in the Army.

"Dixon and I hatched this plan to move to the nearest city, Tucson, and start up a freighting business. He mustered out and we shared a small shack until business picked up. Imagine two long-time army bachelors and a three-year-old."

She laughed. "I'm sure that was a big adjustment."

"It was. Anyway, I grew up in a family of freighters. My father owns M.H. Freighting out of California. The plan when I left California as a young man, was for me to go to University in Georgia, where my father was from, and then come back and take over.

"Of course, the war broke out around the time I finished at university. So, I enlisted as an officer and ended up stationed with the California Column as a cavalry man. We covered the entire southern territories from Fort Leavenworth in Kansas all the way to Fort Yuma in Arizona City and everywhere in between.

"Anyway, I already knew a great deal about freighting and the western territories, especially Arizona. It was the perfect combination of the skills and knowledge needed to create my own company."

Grace smiled. "I'm so sorry for your loss. I understand why you looked my way at Mama's funeral."

"We should head back," he said as they turned around and walked back toward the picnic area.

"How have you been handling the loss of your mother?"

She sighed heavily. "Well enough, I suppose. She had been sick for so long, so my grieving has come in stages. When she could no longer take care of me, I grieved the loss of her energy and involvement. I learned how to invite her into my day by sitting with her after school and telling her my adventures. She and I both came to treasure that time."

He packed up the picnic basket and blanket. Then he helped her into the carriage and headed back into town.

"When we moved here, she improved for a few months. I hoped she would survive long enough to see me marry. But then her health steadily declined. By the time she passed, most of my grieving had too. I was almost relieved that she no longer suffered."

Joshua put his arm around her. She rested her head against his chest.

"I still miss her. Terribly at times. I wish she were still here. She always knew what to say to Daddy to help him see my point of view. She would not be pleased with how he is handling our courtship."

When he pulled to a stop in front of her house, he kissed her on the top of her head and rubbed her arm. "I enjoyed our picnic, despite the somber conversation."

"Me too," she agreed as he led her to the front door.

She turned to face him. He placed his hands on her waist and she moved closer, looping her hands behind his neck. Then he kissed her deeply and she responded. Every time he was with her, he wanted her more and more. He slowed the kiss, reluctant to let her go.

"Please be safe next week," he whispered in her ear.

"I will."

Grace stepped back and he forced his feet to turn around and head home. He needed to find some reason to head down to Camp Date Creek while she was there to make sure she stayed safe.

CHAPTER 21

Grace breathed deeply of the crisp morning air as she rode in the back of Luther Natt's wagon with the medical supplies. Luther had been a doctor during the war. When the war was over, he and his wife, Belinda, headed west to start farming. Belinda had confided in her that they were both eager to leave the horrors of war behind.

When Belinda joined the Women's Aid Society earlier that year, Grace learned of Luther's medical background. The three of them went on one previous trip to render medical aid to the Yuman-Apache at the Camp Date Creek reservation.

As the wagon finished its descent to the valley floor, Grace looked for the place where she and Joshua were stranded. Their broken-down wagon remained where it became useless, though several boards had been pried from it. Likely some travelers used parts of it for firewood.

She scanned the area nearby and found the trees that provided shade for them as they ate fancy sandwiches. The memories of that trip warmed her heart and brought a smile to her face.

Grace knew her heart was already Joshua's. She hoped it was only a matter of time before he asked her to marry him. She already knew her answer.

It was almost midday by the time she and the Natts arrived at Camp Date Creek. Their numbers had increased significantly since she was last there. As far as her eyes could see tents dotted the landscape.

Luther stopped the wagon at the fort to check in with Josephus Williams, the new Indian Agent. When he returned, she asked, "How many are there?"

"Williams said there are around five hundred Yuman-Apache and three hundred Mohave-Apache."

Belinda whispered, "So many."

Luther patted his wife's hand. "We best get started. I think we will be here for a few days. Williams said many are suffering from malaria."

He started the wagon toward the camp and stopped in an open area near the middle. Williams sent an interpreter with them who announced they were healers. In a few short minutes, a long line of sick women and children formed.

Grace sighed as she dug through the first crate, hoping they had enough quinine and other supplies to help these people. Her heart broke over how many needed care. The last time she and the Natts came down to help there had been roughly three hundred Indians. The volume of those in need was staggering.

One by one, Luther examined the sick. Then he showed Grace and Belinda how to care for each one.

A woman around her age ran to the front. She grabbed Grace's arm and tugged, speaking in a language she didn't understand. The interpreter noticed and began translating.

"She says her husband is too sick to stand. She needs help."

"Alright. What is her name?" Grace asked.

"Halapakri."

"Tell her I will follow her." Grace took a vile of quinine and a few other supplies with her.

The woman nodded and took Grace's hand, weaving through the walkways between tents. After several minutes the woman stopped and opened the flap of a tent. Grace ducked her head and entered the small dwelling. The air smelled of sweat and urine.

"Romsa," Halapakri said pointing to the man. Then she said her own name pointing to herself and Romsa pointing to him.

Grace kneeled next to Romsa. Beads of sweat spotted his forehead. She touched it. He was very warm. She started to remove the heavy wool blankets supplied by the Army. Halapakri shook her head. She grabbed her own arms and shook.

"Ah," Grace said, guessing she meant that Romsa had the chills. She had seen these symptoms before. He most likely suffered from malaria.

She poured out a few drops of quinine onto a spoon and placed it on Romsa's lips. The drops slid into his mouth, and he swallowed. Grace acted like she had a mug hoping Halapakri understood she was asking for water. She did and filled a mug with some water, handing it to Grace. Grace spooned the water into Romsa's mouth, and he swallowed each time until it was gone.

Then she looked into Halapakri's dark eyes and smiled. "This will help. He should feel better soon."

"Better," Halapakri replied.

Grace thought she understood the word, but she wasn't sure. She stood and started to leave when Halapakri took her hands and squeezed. She took that to mean the woman was grateful for her help.

As she wound her way back to the wagon, she looked around her. So many people. So many were sick. A few small naked children ran past her. Though the sun was high in the sky and warmed her, in a few hours the temperature would drop. Those children would be too cold.

Grace understood these people lived life in a different way than she did. But she also recognized poverty when she saw it. Back in San Francisco, she remembered turning down an alleyway on her way somewhere. Dirty children huddled against wooden buildings covered with one holey thin blanket. Their faces had been gaunt and their bellies empty. The hopeful look in their eyes was the same look she saw in the Indian children's eyes. They understood she was here to help them.

A tear slid down her cheek and she wiped it away. If it were within her power, there would be no starving children. Alas, it was not. She would continue to do what she could to help these and other poor people. She firmly believed that the blessing of living in a wealthy family was so she could share some of what she had to ease the suffering of others.

When she arrived back at the wagon, she took a long drink from her canteen before joining Belinda.

"Malaria?" she asked.

Grace nodded as Belinda shook her head.

They worked until dusk. Luther moved the wagon inside the fort, and they made camp. After supper, Grace laid down in the back of the wagon and fell asleep quickly.

The next morning, they rose and drove back to the same area by the tents. There seemed to be fewer Indians milling about, but the line for medical attention remained long.

The day never seemed to end. They must have helped a couple of hundred Indians. At the end of the second day, she retired immediately following supper again.

CHAPTER 22

Saturday morning Grace woke to the sounds of fanfare at the fort. General Crook and his aides entered the fort as she and the Natts finished packing up their camp. The soldiers and cavalry men filled the main area of the fort causing a delay in their party leaving.

A major approached and warned them not to go into the Indian camp that day, but the three of them agreed that too many needed their help.

Twenty minutes later, they were set up in the same place as before. Only something was different. Fewer women and children formed a line. The tents seemed eerily quiet compared to the noise from the day before.

Grace finished administering some medicine to a young girl. She handed her a dress, as she had no clothes on. Then she watched as the young girl ran away. She scanned the area. The Yuman-Apache scattered, leaving her and the Natts alone.

"Something's wrong," Luther said as he hurriedly packed up his things.

A loud wail echoed through the camp as hundreds of Indians ran toward the fort. Grace held her breath.

"Let's go!" Luther yelled.

She and Belinda jumped in the back of the wagon as he scurried to the wagon seat and started the horses moving at a fast pace. Shots rang out around them. Smoke filled the air.

Then Grace spotted him. A young boy she recognized from the day before. He could not have been more than four or five years old. He stood crying and looking around frantically. Grace jumped down off the moving wagon, landing with a hard thud. She saw a soldier aim at the little boy. She had to help him.

She hiked up her skirts and ran as fast as she could toward the boy. She scooped him up as she heard the rapport of the rifle. It missed but was followed closely by another. The boy squirmed out of her arms as a third shot fired. She leaped in front of him.

Pain seared through her abdomen. She instinctively grabbed it and looked down. When she pulled her hands away bright red blood covered them. She looked up at the soldier with wide eyes before she collapsed in the dust. The pain was overwhelming.

She thought she heard her name. Gun shots and screams filled the air. She was in someone's arms. He whispered words to her.

"Joshua?"

Then everything went dark.

CHAPTER 23

Joshua woke early Saturday morning at Camp Date Creek. Yesterday he found an excuse to travel down to the reservation, feigning a meeting with Josephus Williams. In truth, he was there to find Grace.

Ever since their picnic, he felt restless. He hated that she planned to be there for several days. When word reached him of numerous Indian attacks, he made sure Victoria would be fine with Miss Bethie. He promised to be back in a few days. Then he packed some things, including his revolver and ammunition. Then he rented a horse from the livery and headed down the mountain. He arrived at Camp Date Creek just after dusk.

He caught a glimpse of Grace as she and her party left the fort that morning.

The hair on the back of his neck stood on end. Something was wrong. General Crook and his men arrived that morning and met with Josephus Williams and the major in charge of the fort. Then they rode out shortly after Grace had.

Joshua mounted his horse and left the fort. He had to find her.

The low rumble of war reached his ears moments before the loud yells of angry natives. Gunfire erupted. Joshua dismounted his horse and slapped its rump, so it ran in the direction of the fort. He dropped to the ground and crawled on his belly as he had done in many a skirmish.

He pulled out his pistol while he scanned the area. He spotted the wagon headed his way. Twenty yards out, Grace jumped off the wagon and his heart lodged in his throat. She was insane!

Joshua stood and ran toward her. The sound of rifle fire echoed from his left. Several shots whizzed by her as she lifted a child into her arms. The child pushed away.

His breath left him as he watched helpless still several feet from her. She clutched her abdomen as bright red blood oozed from a bullet wound and spread across her dress.

"Grace!" Her name left his lungs in a strangled yelp.

He ran full speed toward her as she collapsed to the ground. Gunfire flew by him. A sharp pain in his arm could not stop him.

When he finally reached her, he dropped to his knees. He whispered her name and pressed on the wound. He removed his shirt and tied it tightly around her abdomen where the blood oozed.

"Don't leave me, love."

Then he swept her into his arms and ran through the battlefield toward the fort.

"Joshua?" Her voice was weak.

His heart squeezed and he kept running despite the pain in his arm. Once he was inside the safety of the fort, a soldier took Grace from him and carried her the rest of the way to the post doctor's office.

"Oh, my! Luther, you have to help her," a young woman exclaimed.

The man named Luther fell into step with Joshua headed to the doctor's office. When they arrived, Luther would not let Joshua enter.

"You're injured. Belinda, can you help him?"

The young woman led him to the edge of the porch.

Joshua's heart pounded furiously within his chest. He tried to stand several times, but a soldier came and held him in place as Belinda patched up his arm.

"Looks like you were only grazed," she said, her voice shaky.

"I have to go to Grace."

She nodded and the soldier let him leave.

When he entered the doctor's office, both the post doctor and Luther hovered over Grace.

"We have to get that bullet out," the doctor said.

Joshua watched numbly as they worked on his beloved. He wanted to turn away, but he could not. *Lord, please don't take her.*

After all these years, how many friends had he watched die. He had always been helpless to save them. Several of his men lost their lives in skirmishes with the Indians. Then there was Drew, Hannah's first husband. He stood by while his friend was swallowed up by an avalanche. Then he watched as Hannah lost her first child.

Then there was Rachel, the one that hurt almost as bad as he hurt watching Grace.

She convulsed and two men held her down while Luther fished out the bullet. Joshua's eyes went wide when they cauterized the wound. If she survived, she would have a nasty scar. Blood ran down the table and pooled on the floor. It was not good.

The doctor and Luther finished caring for her and moved on to another patient. Joshua shifted to her side. Her skin looked gray. Her eyes sunken.

Joshua found a chair and sat next to her. He held her hand in his and he stroked her face with the other. A few strands of her golden hair stuck to her forehead, so he smoothed them back.

How cruel it would be to have finally found her only to lose her now.

He coughed trying to hold back the tears.

"Don't leave me, Grace. I love you. I need you."

Joshua rested his head on her arm.

Sometime later, Belinda coaxed him away from Grace, instructing him to get food. She promised she would not leave Grace's side.

Joshua scuffed his feet along the ground with heavy steps as he made his way to the mess hall. He took some food, but his stomach churned too much to eat it.

The scene he witnessed play over and over in his mind. Grace leaping from the wagon to save a little boy. A soldier aimed at the boy.

Wait. A soldier aimed at a child.

When he was in the First Cavalry, the Army directed them to treat women and children as non-combatants. They were not supposed to hurt them whether Indian, Mexican, or white.

Joshua stood and headed directly for Crook's office. He wanted that soldier's head.

He found Crook's men outside of the Indian Agent's office. Joshua pushed through the doors and was immediately tackled by two officers who wrestled him to the ground, smashing his face against the rough floorboards.

"Let him go," General Crook commanded.

The officers took his revolver and searched him for other weapons. When they were satisfied that he could not hurt the general, General Crook offered him a seat and excused his men.

Crook narrowed his eyes as he studied Joshua. His old

military habits surfaced as he realized the impropriety of a captain bursting into a general's quarters.

"You served?" General Crook asked.

Joshua took a deep breath trying to quell his anger. "First Cavalry."

Crook nodded. "You have something you'd like to say?"

"Your men shot women and children. Has the Army's position changed? Are they now considered combatants?"

General Crook took a moment to answer. "They are not."

That was it? Joshua's blood boiled.

"They shot Grace!"

"I am aware of what transpired. I have the soldier in custody."

"Will he be court-martialed?" Joshua demanded.

"That is for me to decide."

Joshua closed his eyes. He was so far over the line. He could lose Grace but needed to calm down before he got himself in trouble.

"We will handle the situation, Mr.?"

"Harrison. Joshua Harrison."

"We will handle it."

Crook called for his officers to enter the room. They escorted Joshua from the building.

The reality of what happened knocked the air from his lungs. His stomach churned and he wretched. He wiped his mouth on the back of his hand.

A soldier offered him a shirt. He forgot he used his to help save Grace. Then he made his way back to the doctor's office.

Belinda let him have the chair. She left and brought back some water. He took it and drank.

"Grace," he whispered. "I love you so completely. If you

make it," his voice cracked. "I promise I will make you my wife soon. Just don't leave me."

Later in the evening, Luther and Belinda pressured him to leave Grace's side. They fed him and gave him a place to lay his head. He fell asleep in the back of their wagon.

CHAPTER 24

The next morning, Joshua woke and went to Grace's side without breakfast. When Luther and Belinda entered, he asked them if they could take her home.

Luther agreed that slow mountain climb in the wagon should be fine. So, Joshua arranged a place for her in the back of the wagon. He carried Grace out to it and lovingly laid her down. Then he took a seat next to her, never letting go of her hand.

The trip seemed painfully slow as his mind haunted him. He should not have let her go. But he had no say over what she did or where she went. Even if he did, he could not really stop her. She was made to help others. Stopping her would kill her soul.

The voice in his mind accused him of failure. It taunted him.

Until they came upon the remnants of the wagon where he first kissed Grace. He looked over and found the trees. A half smile curved his lips as he remembered how beautiful she looked when he rescued her from the creek. Even though she had been drenched, she was the most beautiful woman he had ever seen.

That day when she looked up at him, he saw for the first time a woman who wanted him. Him. The complete failure at matters of the heart. The man who other women had seen as a loyal friend. Grace saw him as something more from the very beginning.

They loved each other. Though neither said the words aloud, it was there just under the surface of every touch, every kiss, every gaze. He loved her with his whole heart, and she loved him.

The thought of losing her pierced his heart afresh. *Please, Lord, do not take her.*

The sway of the wagon lulled him to sleep until it stopped in front of her home. He thanked Luther and Belinda. Then he gathered Grace into his arms as Luther untied Joshua's borrowed horse from the back of the wagon and looped the reins over the hitching post.

Joshua pounded on the front door. Kingsley greeted him and then when white when he saw Grace in his arms.

"This way, Mr. Harrison," he said as he led the way upstairs to Grace's room.

Joshua tenderly laid her in her bed. Then he sat on the edge of it.

The maid entered the room. A man touched his shoulder.

"You need to go home, Mr. Harrison." Kingsley's voice was full of compassion. "Before Mr. Talbert sees you."

Kingsley ushered him out the front door. Joshua stared at the gate. The street. The horse. His heart remained in Grace's room, even if his body must move forward.

He took the reins and walked aimlessly.

"Cap!" Dixon's voice broke through his fog.

He was outside of the freight office. Dixon took the reins from his hands and secured the horse, then he led Joshua into the office in the back.

"You can't go home looking like that. You'll give Victoria a fright."

"Victoria," Joshua whispered.

"Hang tight. You just stay here, and I'll run and get you a fresh set of clothes."

Joshua nodded.

Sometime later, Dixon returned and made sure Joshua changed. Then he walked his friend home.

"Papa!" Victoria greeted him and ran to hug him but stopped short. "What's wrong?"

Dixon spoke up. "Miss Talbert was hurt. So was your papa, but he'll be alright. He just needs to rest."

Dixon led him upstairs to his room and told him to lie down. Joshua obeyed. Sleep enveloped him.

Sometime later Joshua woke. His mind was foggy. Slowly the images of Grace came back to him. She had been shot. He needed to go to her.

"Hold your horses, Cap." Dixon pushed him back down on the bed. "You ain't going anywhere. Stop being stubborn and rest, would ya?"

Joshua rolled over on his side showing his back to Dixon, frustrated that he could not go to Grace.

The next day Joshua went to work but could not concentrate on the papers before him. He left his office and walked to Grace's home.

When he knocked on the door, Kingsley answered. "Mr. Harrison."

"May I see Grace?"

"I'm sorry sir, but Mr. Talbert will not allow it."

Joshua walked away dejected.

Each day for a week, he tried again. Each day Kingsley refused to let him in but did tell him more about how she was doing.

Finally on September fifteenth, he learned that she had been awake for a few days.

"Has she asked for me?"

Kingsley evaded the question. "Mr. Talbert—"

"Yes, I know."

He turned and headed back to the office. He needed to see her. He needed to talk to her.

That afternoon, Dixon and Perry pulled up behind the freight office with a full load. Joshua helped unload the heavy crates. The physical labor provided a good distraction for a few minutes.

"How's Miss Talbert?" Dixon asked.

Joshua shrugged.

Dixon frowned. "He still won't let you see her?"

"No."

"That ain't right."

No, it wasn't. Joshua wracked his brain trying to think of some way to get a message to her. Perhaps her friend Caroline could speak with her.

He went back into his office and composed a short note. Then he headed over to the Anderson's home and enlisted Caroline's help. She promised to let him know how she fared.

It was almost supper time, so he waited at home, pacing the length of the parlor.

Finally at half past seven, Caroline arrived.

"She is doing well. I was not able to give her your note. Her father hovered in the doorway eavesdropping the entire time. She is recovering. I think she wanted to ask about you, but her father only allowed me a minute alone with her before he sat down in the chair by her bed."

"Thank you."

"I'm sorry I could not do more to help you."

Joshua sighed. He would find a way. Simon Talbert could not hide his daughter away forever.

CHAPTER 25

Grace woke. Her brain was foggy, and her body ached.

"Miss Grace!" Mercy exclaimed. "How are you feeling?"

When she tried to sit, pain tore through her lower abdomen. Mercy helped her, propping several more pillows behind her. As she leaned back, she winced.

"Are you in pain? I can mix up some willow bark tea."

Grace nodded.

As Mercy started to leave, Grace asked, "What happened?"

"I'll let Mr. Talbert know you are awake." Then Mercy's footfalls on the stairs echoed up to her room.

She closed her eyes. Her head pounded.

"Grace," her daddy said.

She opened her eyes.

"What happened?"

Daddy kissed her on the top of her head. Then he took a seat in the chair next to her and held her hand—a scene too familiar at her mama's bedside. Her heart ached. She wished Mama was here.

"You were down at that awful reservation with your friends. Those wretched Indians attacked General Crook. They tried to kill him. You were caught in the crossfire and shot."

Flashes from that day played in her mind. A little boy. A

soldier pointed a rifle at him. Fierce pain.

She placed a hand over the gunshot wound.

"Mr. Harrison brought you home."

"Joshua was not with me. Only the Natts and I were there."

Daddy frowned. "I'm telling you what Kingsley told me. It was Mr. Harrison who brought you home."

She remembered falling to the ground. Someone picked her up and carried her. Could Joshua really have been there?

"How long ago?" she whispered.

"You were shot six days ago and arrived home five days ago."

Daddy stroked her hand.

Mercy arrived with the willow bark tea. Grace slowly sipped the bitter liquid.

"Has Joshua stopped by?"

"No, that man has not been here." Daddy's eyebrows dipped until they almost touched leaving deep rows in his forehead. He was not telling her something.

"I'm feeling tired," she said when she finished her tea.

She closed her eyes and fell asleep.

Sometime later she heard voices echo up from the entryway.

"I… see her…"

"Sorry… Harrison…"

She strained to hear more, but exhaustion pulled her under again.

A few days later, when she woke, Grace felt restless. The staff continued to dodge her questions about Joshua. She was certain he had been by, but everyone, Father included, continued to deny that he had been.

That afternoon, she asked Mercy to draw her a bath. She had lost track of the days. It had to be almost two weeks since her trip.

When the water was ready, Mercy helped her into the tub and waited outside the doorway, in case Grace needed anything. She studied the angry black and red mark on her abdomen to the right of her belly button a few inches down. When the doctor came by that morning, he told her she had been fortunate that the bullet did not damage her bowels. However, he was concerned about the location of the injury. He thought she might not be able to have children.

Tears trickled down her cheeks. She had so much love to give. She wanted children. She knew Joshua would want children too. Would he still want her if there was a chance she could not fulfill that dream for him?

Her tears turned to sobs.

"Miss Grace?" Mercy called from the doorway. "Are you alright?"

"I'm... fine." She lied.

How dreadful that in her attempt to save a child she may have lost her only hope of having her own. She shook off the thought. Doctor said he did not know for certain one way or the other. She needed to stop borrowing trouble.

She scrubbed the dirt and grime from her skin, then she called for Mercy to help her out of the tub. It hurt to stand. She managed to hold herself together while she dried off. Mercy slipped a fresh nightgown over her head and helped her back to bed.

Fatigue washed over her in waves, begging her to sleep.

The next day, Caroline Anderson paid her a visit. Daddy was home and he lingered around them. She wanted to ask Caroline about Joshua, but Daddy would not leave.

For another week, Grace settled into a routine. Each morning when she woke, Mercy helped her walk around her room. She helped Grace groom and then led her back to bed to sleep more.

One afternoon she spotted Kingsley lurking in the doorway.

"Kingsley."

"Yes, Miss Grace."

"Please come in." She shifted so she could see him better.

"I am glad to see you much improved," Kingsley said.

"Thank you. Tell me, has Joshua been by yet?"

Kingsley's eyes shifted to the corner of the room. "I cannot say, Miss Grace."

She frowned. "Cannot or will not?"

He looked at her. His normally stoic face contorted as he opened and closed his mouth several times.

"Out with it," she said firmly.

He cleared his throat. "Yes, Mr. Harrison has stopped by nearly every day."

Grace sucked in a sharp breath. "Every day? And why have my eyes not seen him?"

Kingsley looked away.

She straightened her back and held her head high. "Do I need to remind you of your station?" she asked as she narrowed her eyes.

"No, Miss Grace."

Still, he did not answer.

"Answer me."

His shoulders sagged. "Mr. Talbert instructed me not to permit Mr. Harrison to enter the house."

Her blood boiled and she threw back the covers.

"Mercy!" she yelled.

Kingsley started to leave.

"I am not done with you yet." She turned flashing eyes on her father's butler.

"Miss Grace, you called for me?" Mercy asked.

"Get my light green house dress."

"Yes, Miss Grace."

She turned towards Kingsley. "You will go to Joshua's office at once and bring him back here. You will let him into this house. I will be waiting for him in the parlor."

Kingsley started to object.

"Now!" She cut him off. Heaven help her if she did not sound like her father in that moment.

What Father did was unconscionable. She could only imagine how hurt Joshua felt. She was not sure how much time had passed. It had to be two or three weeks. She only hoped he knew that her father had done that. Not her.

Mercy helped her into her light green house dress. Then she brushed out Grace's hair until it shown.

"Do you want me to put it up?" Mercy asked.

"No. Let's just pull back the sides with a comb. I don't feel up to much primping."

"Yes, Miss Grace."

When she was presentable, she instructed Mercy to help her into the parlor. It seemed so far away. The stairs left her winded and she was grateful for Mercy's assistance as she reclined on the chaise near the fireplace. She shivered. Mercy lit a fire.

"That will be all for now. Have Esther bring in tea for two when Mr. Harrison arrives."

The maid curtsied and left the room.

Graced leaned her head back on the chaise, worn out from the trek down the stairs. She could not fault Kingsley for obeying her father's orders, for he was father's butler. Mama never would have stood for such behavior from Father. Times like that made her miss her even more.

She would close her eyes for a few moments before

Joshua arrived.

CHAPTER 26

Joshua tried and failed to shake off his melancholy. Every day he tried to visit Grace and every day the butler denied him entry. At least the man told him how she was doing. Regardless, he needed to see her with his own eyes.

The bell rang from the counter. Joshua set aside the newspaper and made his way to the customer area.

"Mrs. Atwood," he greeted the dressmaker.

Ira popped his head in and left when he saw Joshua answered the call.

"I have a large shipment waiting in San Francisco. I was hoping you could help."

He listened to her request. Then he started some paperwork. His hand froze when he recognized Kingsley walking past the front window.

He called back to Ira to complete Mrs. Atwood's request. Then he hurried to greet the butler outside.

"Mr. Harrison."

"Kingsley." Joshua spat out the name.

"Miss Grace instructed me to bring you at once."

His heart raced at the sound of her name.

"Is she alright?" Joshua asked as he walked next to Kingsley.

"Other than being vexed at me, she is fine." The butler cleared his throat. "I owe you an apology, Mr. Harrison. I was following Mr. Talbert's orders. Still, I could have done more to aid your cause."

Joshua thanked him and walked the rest of the way in silence. He wanted to run to her side, to hold her in his arms and proclaim his love for her. He missed her the past few weeks. It had been torturous to be apart and know so little.

All the fears he had started to melt away. She had not rejected him. She asked for him. She wanted to see him.

When Kingsley led him into the parlor, he was unprepared for the sight. Grace reclined in a chaise near the fire. Her skin looked pale. She lost weight and looked too thin in her loose light green dress. Her eyes were closed and her breathing soft. Her long golden hair rested on one side of her body cascading to her waist.

"Miss Grace," Kingsley said quietly as he touched her shoulder. "Mr. Harrison is here for you."

Her beautiful gray-blue eyes fluttered open. "Thank you. Have Esther bring the tea now."

His heart ached. She looked so frail.

She patted a spot next to her on the chaise. In two heartbeats he was next to her. He could not speak around the lump lodged in his throat. He brushed a few wayward strands of hair back from her face.

"Joshua." She said his name on a breath. He searched her eyes and saw the truth there. She loved him fully and completely.

A tear ran down the side of his face. She was safe and on the mend.

She opened her arms. "Come here."

He did as she bade. She held him so close. Her hair smelled of lilac and he breathed deeply.

The sound of a teapot clattered on a metal tray, and he leaned back.

"Miss Grace," the older woman said as she set the tea tray on a table next to them.

"Thank you, Esther."

She turned her gaze to him. "I'm sorry I am not much of a hostess today. Would you mind terribly? Two lumps, please."

He poured her a cup of tea and dropped in two cubes of sugar. Then he stirred it until the sugar dissolved, still unable to speak for the rush of emotions clogging his heart. Then he handed her the tea.

Grace smiled at him. "I have missed you. I am so sorry for what Father did. I wish I had known sooner."

Joshua poured himself a cup of tea and took a sip. "I sent Caroline with a note a week or so ago. She mentioned your father would not leave you the entire time."

"Yes. I tried to ask about you, but he would not give us a minute alone."

"You scared me half to death, you know," he said before taking another sip of tea. "You leaped off that wagon in the middle of a battle."

His voice cracked and he took another sip of tea.

"I saw the whole thing. You saved that boy by taking a bullet in your gut."

Her hand shook dribbling tea on her dress. He took the cup from her and set both his and hers on the tray.

"I thought my mind was confused. Father seemed to think you were there, but you did not travel with us."

Joshua looked down and gave her a sheepish grin. "I sorta made up an excuse to travel to make sure you were safe. I arrived too late to find you the first night. The next morning the battle broke out."

He reached up and caressed her cheek. He wanted to ask her to marry him. Yet then was not the right time, nor the way he wished to do so.

"Kiss me," she whispered.

He pulled her to him and wrapped his arms around her tightly. Then he lowered his lips to hers, gently searching and teasing. She felt weak in his arms. That did not stop her from returning his kiss. He loved that woman. He gently and sweetly ended the kiss, letting her settle against the chaise again.

The door of the house flew open. Simon Talbert stormed into the room.

"Get out of my house!"

Joshua leaped to his feet.

"Daddy," Grace said softly.

"Not a word," he yelled at her before he turned his attention back to Joshua.

"Get out."

"Daddy, I invited him here."

"I don't care. He needs to leave."

Joshua stood his ground and did not move. Not even when Simon Talbert moved closer and poked him in the chest. Joshua grabbed his hand and threw it way from him.

"Father!" Grace yelled as she stood up. She gripped the back of the chaise so hard her knuckles turned white. "Stop it!"

"He is no good for you, Grace. I told you before to stop seeing him."

"I will not. I am old enough to choose as I see fit. And I see fit to choose Joshua."

Joshua's heart soared to the sky and back as her words healed a broken part of his heart.

Simon growled and stormed out of the house.

Grace moaned and started to fall. Joshua caught her and helped her back onto the chaise. She wilted against the piece of furniture as the fight left her.

"I'm sorry," she whispered. "He won't let this go."

"Does it change how you feel about me?"

"Not in the slightest." She gave him a weak smile. "I love you, Joshua Harrison. But I'm very tired now." Her eyes closed as she relaxed in sleep.

"I love you, Grace Talbert. One day soon, I will ask you. I promise." He kissed her forehead and left; his heart full.

———

Grace missed Joshua leaving. She wished she had more energy to spend time with him. Mercy woke her for supper.

"Is Father home?" she asked.

"Yes, Miss Grace."

For a few seconds she considered going upstairs to avoid him. "Help me to the dining room?"

Mercy walked slowly next to her until they reached the dining room. Then she held a chair for Grace. Grace melted onto the chair.

Father sat in his chair at the head of the table. Mercy dished her up a plate. Father dished his own. Grace bowed her head and said a silent prayer of gratitude before she ate. Though Father did not take kindly to praying, he always waited for her and Mama to say their prayers.

"You must stop seeing that man."

Grace sighed, wishing she had fled upstairs after all. There was nothing her father could do or say that would deter her from seeing or even one day marrying Joshua. How she hoped that would happen.

When she did not respond, he slammed his fork and knife down on the table. She jumped, then calmly set her silverware down.

"Are you listening to me?"

"I hear you, Father. The neighbors hear you."

"Then you will stop seeing him?"

"No."

She picked up her knife and fork and began eating again.

He glared at her. In the past she would have capitulated. No longer.

"I am past the age of consent. I do not need your permission to choose who I will court or even who I marry. While I would dearly love for you to try to get along with the man I choose, I will not alter my decision based on your lonely tantrum."

He stood and slapped her face. "Do not speak to me with such disrespect."

Kingsley flinched and moved closer to her.

Her face stung as much as her heart did. Father had never struck her. Not once.

Kingsley cleared his throat and Father sat down.

"Father, do not strike me again."

"Don't disobey me again."

"If we are to live under the same roof, now that Mama has passed on and can no longer sway your opinion," she said, "we must come to an agreement. You will never lay a hand on me again."

"You do not threaten me."

"You are correct. I am not threatening you. However, there are behaviors I will not abide, nor would have Mama. Striking me is one of them."

Kingsley put himself between them as she watched her father's temper boil over. Kingsley pretended to refill Father's full wine glass until Father motion him away.

"I will not strike you again."

She resisted the urge to rub her stinging cheek, lest she give her father the satisfaction that he wounded her heart so deeply. It hurt far more that her relationship crumbled bit by bit each day.

Exhaustion pulled at her, and she set her silverware aside. She called for Mercy, but it was Kingsley who assisted her upstairs.

"Would you like me to have Mercy bring a tray up?" he asked.

"No. I will just rest now."

She saw a half-formed apology on the butler's face as he pulled the door closed.

As she closed her eyes, she worried about how far Father would go to stop her from being with Joshua.

CHAPTER 27

The next week, Joshua stood in front of Grace's home. She had sent word that she felt well enough for a calm outing. Kingsley allowed him into the house without hesitation. Grace descended the stairs slowly, wearing a dark emerald green dress with a bustle and a matching hat. She smiled when she saw him, and his heart flipped upside down. Pink colored the apples of her cheeks.

He led her outside to the carriage and helped her up. When he sat next to her, he let out a loud sigh.

"Are you well?" he asked.

"I am now that I'm out of Father's house for a few hours. Did I tell you he struck me at supper the night you last visited?"

Joshua's jaw tightened. "What happened?"

"I'm sorry to say he is dead set against our relationship. I stood up to him respectfully, though he did not see it that way."

She looked towards the sidewalk along the street. "He's not done that before or since. I wonder, looking back on my life, if he always had such a temper or if Mama somehow managed to tame it from him when he was around me."

Joshua sat up straighter and held the reins tightly. "If you are concerned, you come to me. I will not allow him to touch you again."

Grace sighed. "In a way, I think he knows he is losing me to you. Somehow, he feels threatened. What he doesn't understand is that I have plenty of room in my heart for the both of you."

He clenched his jaw so tight he thought he might break a tooth. If Simon Talbert hurt her again, he would answer to Joshua. He understood Grace's desire to maintain some relationship with her father. It was unfortunate that her father placed so many conditions on that relationship.

"Will he throw you out?"

"I don't think so. At this point, it would not matter. I can manage my own trust fund as well as make my own decisions. I do not need a fancy house or servants." She giggled, "Although I do like my fancy clothes and fancy sandwiches."

He snorted. "I know you do."

Within minutes, he pulled the carriage to a stop in front of his home. He helped her down and escorted her into the house.

"Miss Grace," Victoria greeted her with a hug and a kiss on the cheek. "You look well."

Grace laughed so carefree compared to their earlier conversation. "I feel well. You look lovely this evening. Is that a new dress?"

"Yes, I was saving it for today."

Grace shot him a raised eyebrow.

"She also hit another growth spurt. All her dresses were a few inches too short. Can't have my daughter running around with exposed ankles."

"The scandal." Grace feigned shock. "Smells good."

"Have a seat here with Victoria. I have a few more finishing touches."

He headed into the kitchen and lit the candles on the table. Then he pulled the roast, potatoes, and carrots from the oven and placed them on a serving dish. He double checked the table to make sure everything was perfect.

"Papa let Miss Bethie have the night off. Her sister Caroline is having a hard time."

"Oh? Is something wrong with Caroline?"

"No. She is four months along according to Miss Bethie. She's been sick a lot so Miss Bethie thought it would be nice to help her out tonight."

Joshua smiled. It was a convenient excuse. He really wanted Victoria and Grace to himself that night.

He stood in the doorway of the parlor and rubbed his hands together. "Supper is ready."

Grace smiled and joined him. When she turned the corner, she gasped. "It's lovely."

Exactly the response he was hoping for. The candles lit the highlights of her hair giving it a golden glow.

"These flowers are beautiful. Where did you find so many roses this time of year?"

"I'm not giving away my source." Martha Stanton's garden rivaled the botanical gardens in the east.

He held out a chair for her. Then he did the same for Victoria before he took a seat across from Grace. He took both their hands and prayed.

"Lord, we thank you for this special woman and this special night. We ask you to bless this food and our time together. Thank you for your bountiful grace. Amen."

Grace held onto his hand for a few seconds longer. "Special?"

He winked at her. "Do you think I would make my world-famous pot roast for just anyone?"

She laughed.

"You make it for me, Papa."

"Well, Pumpkin, you are not just anyone."

He held out his hand for Grace's plate. Then he dished up a fair-sized helping, reminding himself she's a lady. He dished up some for Victoria and himself.

"Dig in."

"Mmm," she said. "I taste rosemary and garlic. This is good."

"You don't have to sound so surprised."

"And you made this, not Miss Bethie?" she asked.

Joshua smiled and nodded. He was enjoying the game.

"Papa used to make this all the time when Uncle Dixon lived with us in Tucson."

Grace looked his way.

"It's all true. Same recipe that my mama made. She taught me a few things about cooking. The rest I picked up on the trail in the Army."

"You'll have to thank her for me."

Joshua laughed. "I hope to tell her that her world-famous pot roast stole my lady's heart."

"Oh, it has."

He grew nervous as he ate. He planned the night carefully and once it arrived, he felt awkward. He patted his pocket to make sure the ring was still there.

Victoria smiled at him. He told her shortly before he left to pick up Grace what he was going to do. She wholeheartedly approved.

Grace yawned and suddenly looked very tired.

"Are you alright?" he asked, taking her hand.

"Just a little tired. It has been a long time since I've been out."

"Do you want me to take you home?"

"Not yet."

He blew out a long breath. Then he stood to clear away the dishes.

"I'll start the dishes, Papa." Victoria nodded her head toward the parlor.

He held back a laugh. She really was fine with the plan.

Joshua took Grace's hand and led her into the parlor to one of the chairs by the fire. Then he scooted another chair close and held both her hands in his.

"Grace, I think you know this already. I love you with all my heart. I think I have loved you from the first moment I saw—"

A knock sounded at the door. He hesitated annoyed that someone was wrecking his perfect moment.

"I'll get it," Victoria said as she hurried to the door.

He watched to see who it was.

"You must be Victoria," a woman spoke with a lilting Irish accent. "I am your Aunt Keira."

"Victoria, go upstairs," Joshua said. He dropped Grace's hands and hurried to the front door, stopping the woman from entering.

He turned back to look at Grace. "One moment."

Then he stepped onto the front porch.

"Who are you?"

A man with shocking red hair and a thick Irish accent answered. "I'm Collin Brannan and this is my wife Keira, Rachel's sister."

The breath left Joshua's lungs and he staggered as if the man had punched him hard in the gut.

"We're here for Victoria," Keira said.

"She is my daughter now."

"If yar last name is Feagan. But 'tis not, is it Mr. Harrison?"

Joshua's stomach churned. He could not believe it.

"I'm her closest kin and I have a right to take her."

Think. Think. He had papers. Legal papers that proved Victoria was his. The Brannans could not show up on his doorstep and try to take away his daughter. Not without a fight.

"Leave now," he demanded.

"Aye," Collin said. "But we'll be back in the marnin'."

Joshua stood to his full height and crossed his arms over his chest. "Go."

The Brannans turned and walked down the street.

He let out a huge breath and coughed as his stomach threatened to expel his supper.

"Joshua," Grace's soft voice came from behind him. "Come back inside."

He did.

She took a seat by the fire while he paced the length of the parlor.

"How much did you hear?"

"Enough to know that we need to speak to Alex Glassman first thing in the morning."

Joshua pointed his hand to his chest. "I have papers. I… She's my *daughter*. Grace, they can't take her away."

He dropped to his knees in front of her and rested his head in her lap.

CHAPTER 28

Grace's heart twisted over what she heard. These strangers showing up out of the blue threatening to take Victoria away. It wreaked of the low-life despicable things Father was capable of.

When Joshua fell to his knees, he rested his head on her lap. She stroked his hair as he wept.

"Papa?" Victoria peeked down from the top of the stairs. "Is that woman really my aunt?"

He motioned for her to come to him. When she did, he held her tight. Grace could barely breathe watching the love he had for his daughter and the sheer terror at the thought of losing her.

"I don't know, Pumpkin."

"Are the horses still out front?" Grace asked.

He nodded.

"And is Dixon in town?"

He nodded again.

"Then I will go fetch him."

"No." Joshua stood. "You are still recovering. Stay here and I'll go."

"Very well. Victoria, would you come sit beside me?"

"Yes, Miss Grace."

While Joshua was gone, Grace did her best to distract Victoria from the upsetting news. The moment the door opened Victoria ran to Joshua.

Grace tried to stifle a yawn, but Dixon caught her.

"Miss Talbert, how are you?"

She warned him with a glare. "I'm fine. Ready to support Joshua in any way I can." It was a half lie. She was weary to the bone.

"Dixon, can you watch Victoria while I take Grace home?" Joshua asked.

He agreed.

"Come," he said before he led her out to the carriage.

In the light from the streetlamps, she saw him chew his lower lip.

"Joshua, look at me."

He looked straight ahead.

"Look at me."

When he did her heart broke. He looked like a wounded animal caught in a trap that he could not free himself from. That was exactly the type of thing her father would do. Strip a man of everything he loved in order to exact his will on that man. She heard plenty of stories about her father's dealings.

"In the morning, let's go to Alex. He will tell you what can be done legally. Until then, try not to worry."

He pulled the carriage to a stop in front of her house. When he came around to her side of the carriage, she hesitated.

"Give me your hands. We need to pray."

She closed her eyes and bowed her head. "Lord, we know you are in control of the world and everything in it. Dark forces have brought this devastating news to Joshua's doorstep. We pray for peace and for wisdom in this crisis. We know that you will go before us, and you surround us. In Jesus's name. Amen."

When she looked up, she saw Joshua swipe a hand over his eyes. He helped her down from the carriage and walked her to the door. He pulled her close and she wrapped her arms around him.

"This was not how tonight was supposed to go."

His voice sounded far away.

"It was supposed to be…"

Special, she thought. It was supposed to be the night he proposed. She was sure that was the direction the night had been headed before the unexpected visitors showed up.

"It will be alright. Trust God, Joshua."

She reached up and placed a hand on his cheek.

"Trust him."

When he nodded, she turned and went inside. She felt ready to collapse as all her energy faded. Mercy helped her upstairs and as she got ready for bed.

Mercy turned down the light as Grace snuggled under the covers.

"Mercy?"

"Yes, Miss Grace."

"Can you have Kingsley send word to Alex Glassman that Joshua and I will need to meet with him first thing in the morning."

"Yes, Miss Grace."

After Mercy left, tears streamed down her face. *Lord, please don't take Victoria away from him. It will break him.*

CHAPTER 29

The next morning, Grace waited in the parlor for Joshua. He was sure he looked a fright, having slept only a few hours. Miss Bethie came home late last night, and he had filled her in. She promised she would keep Victoria home from school and keep a close eye out for any trouble.

His heart ached and his stomach churned.

"Ready?" he asked, not even attempting a smile.

She kissed his cheek. "It will be alright. Alex will help."

Joshua was not so confident.

He helped her into the carriage and drove them to the solicitor's office in silence.

When they entered the law office, Mr. Whitaker greeted them and showed them to the parlor.

"Good morning, Grace, Mr. Harrison," Alex Glassman greeted them stoically.

Joshua argued with himself all last night if he should trust Grace's former suitor. Or if Glassman blamed him in any way for their breakup.

Alex showed them to his office and offered them a seat before sitting on the other side of the darkly stained walnut desk. He turned to Grace.

"I received your note that you have an urgent legal matter."

"Thank you for seeing us," Grace said. "Joshua is the one

in need. I am here for moral support."

Joshua cleared his throat and explained the unexpected appearance of a woman and man claiming to be Victoria's relatives.

"This Keira Brannan stated her intention to take Victoria," Joshua said.

"And how did Victoria come to live with you?"

Joshua shifted under Glassman's scrutiny. "I knew her mother when I was stationed at Fort Goodwin as part of the First Cavalry. Her mother, Rachel Feagan, nursed me back to health after an Indian attack. Victoria was three at the time."

"What happened to Rachel Feagan?" Alex asked, taking down several notes.

"She was killed by the same band of Indians several months later. My patrol came upon her just before she passed. She asked me to take Victoria."

Joshua explained the whole story of how he mustered out and he and Dixon started the freight company.

"Did you formally adopt her?"

"Yes, when she was six, I worked with an attorney down in Tucson. Virgil Pittman."

"I know him. He drew up the papers then?"

"Yes. I have them if you'd like to examine them." Joshua handed over the adoption papers.

Alex Glassman studied the papers for several minutes while Joshua held his breath. Grace reached over and held his hand.

"These are legitimate. You are undeniably Victoria's father and legal guardian."

Joshua let out his breath, thankful that Dixon hounded him all those years ago to make sure he did the paperwork.

"However," Glassman started. Joshua's stomach tightened. "If this couple takes you to court, they could try to present a case that paints you as an unfit father—"

"Alex, Joshua is a good father," Grace said glaring at him.

"I am not saying otherwise. I'm simply trying to prepare him for what could happen in court." Alex turned his focus back to Joshua. "I will need to know everything. Anything that they could possibly use against you, no matter how insignificant it seems."

He stood and opened the door. "Bradley, clear my schedule."

Then he returned to his seat behind the desk.

"One other point, before we start going over your history. Your case would be stronger if you were married. The court is often more favorable towards a couple than a single parent."

Joshua's heart squeezed.

"Joshua, I could—" Grace started.

"Could you give us a minute?" he asked Alex.

Alex nodded and left the room.

"I would marry you," Grace said.

He frowned. He wanted to marry her—had been about to ask her last night when they were interrupted.

"I want to marry you, Grace, but not like this. Not so I can keep my daughter and potentially have you resent me for the rest of our marriage."

"I would not resent you."

"Please, Grace, let me lead us. Allow me to propose properly at the right time and in the right way."

She nodded.

"Now, I think you should leave." He could not parade a list of all his potential failings as a father in front of her. It would be bad enough to live through it in court.

"I want to stay. To be here for you."

He placed a hand on her cheek. "You look weary. You are still recovering. Please go home and rest. And pray."

"Alright," she conceded at last.

He escorted her to the front door. Bradley volunteered to drive her home in the carriage and then dropped off the horses and carriage at the livery.

Joshua followed Glassman back into his office.

"Tell me everything. I cannot prepare arguments in your defense if you hide or lie."

Joshua nodded. Over the next several hours, Glassman grilled him, and Joshua confessed. He told him about his last housekeeper in Tucson, Carmella and what he learned of her character. That was the most damaging of his failures.

"What do you know about Rachel's family?"

"Not much. She was married to a Mr. Feagan. I do not know his first name. She was already widowed by the time I met her in 1865."

"Did she ever mention a sister?"

Joshua shook his head. "She never mentioned anything about her family or his. I just assumed there was no family since she asked me to take care of Victoria as my own."

"Were those her exact words?"

"Yes."

Alex jotted down more notes.

"I'll be honest, it depends on the judge how a case could go. Judge Hezekiah Stanton is your best chance. He and his wife adopted a young Indian orphan several years back. I believe he would be the most sympathetic to your cause."

"Can we ask for a specific judge?" Joshua asked not knowing anything about a case like this.

"Unfortunately, no."

Alex set his elbows on his desk, tented his fingers, and

leaned forward. "I think it would help your cause if you married Grace."

"I'm surprised you would say that. Didn't you court her for some length of time?"

"Over eight months." Alex relaxed in his chair and looked at the corner of the room. "She was right. We did not love each other. When I accepted that it did not bother me that she seemed taken with you so quickly."

Joshua shifted in his seat. Nothing about that conversation was comfortable.

"Just think about it."

When his stomach growled, he glanced at his pocket watch. It was nearly three o'clock.

"If there's nothing else," Joshua said as he stood.

Alex walked him to the door. "I'll let the court know that I'm representing you so they will contact me about a case. *If* they even decide to pursue legal action."

"Thank you."

Joshua left the law office. He took a deep breath of the fresh fall air, then let it out slowly. What a nightmare.

He went straight to Grace's house to update her.

"What happened?" she asked.

"Do you feel up for a walk to the café? I haven't eaten anything all day."

He offered his arm, and she took it. The walk to the café only took a few minutes. She seemed winded and he kicked himself for not getting a carriage.

After they ordered some food, he filled her in.

"Alex thinks they might have a case. He thinks Judge Stanton would rule in my favor but tells me we cannot request a specific judge."

"I will pray we get Judge Stanton."

Joshua took her hand. "I know you want to help." He

cleared his throat. "I'm embarrassed to say, I have made a few significant mistakes raising Victoria. The most recent was hiring such a terrible housekeeper back in January, while we were still in Tucson. I am not sure I want you hearing about all my failures."

"Joshua, there is nothing anyone could say that would make me think less of you."

His heart swelled in his chest.

"I want to be by your side. If you plan to marry me one day, I want you to look back on this trial and remember that I was here for you."

He smiled as his throat clogged with emotion.

When they finished the meal, he walked her home. Then he headed to his home to wait for what might come.

CHAPTER 30

Grace asked Kingsley to call for a carriage to take her to Caroline Larson's home. She also asked him to send a message to Rebecca Quinn to join her there. The carriage driver helped her down.

When she knocked on the door, Helen Larson answered.

"Caroline is expecting you. Rebecca is already here. Come on back."

Grace frowned. "Is Caroline alright?"

"Yes. The doctor ordered bed rest for her until the baby comes in February. I moved in to help out," Helen explained.

"That's still four months away."

"The doctor was confident if Caroline takes it easy, both she and the baby will be fine."

"Is that Grace?" Caroline called from her bedroom.

Helen showed her to Caroline's room.

Grace leaned over and hugged her friend. "When did all this come about?"

"Two days ago. I knew you were still recovering, and I didn't want to worry you."

"Caroline," Rebecca said, stretching her name out with her delightful southern accent. "We both would have come had you told us."

"I know. But you're here now. I'm glad for the company."

Caroline motioned for Grace to sit in a chair to her right. Rebecca was in a chair to her left.

"What happened, Grace, that you called us together?" Caroline asked.

Grace looked at the corner of the room. "I wish I could claim this was purely a social visit, but you are correct, something terrible has happened."

She told them everything she knew about the Brannans' mysterious appearance in Joshua's life and how they wanted to take Victoria away.

"My goodness!" Rebecca exclaimed. "Have you sent him to Alexander?"

"Yes, we were there yesterday morning. Joshua was going back over again today. He received word late yesterday that the Brannans are petitioning the court for custody."

"Oh, no!" Caroline held out her hand to Grace. Grace took her hand.

She looked down at the floor. "I just can't shake the feeling that Father is behind all this."

"Whatever do you mean?" Rebecca asked.

"It seems very odd that within a week of a terrible argument with Father that for no reason at all, Victoria's long lost relatives appear. If they are even her relatives."

She sighed. "Father does not like Joshua. I think it is because he did not choose him. Or maybe he wants to hold on to me because he fears being alone. I don't know."

"What did Alexander say?" Rebecca asked. Grace found it interesting how her friend was the only person who called him by his full name. She held on to propriety from their upbringing, she supposed.

"He thinks Joshua will have a better case if he is married."

The room grew silent. Caroline lifted a finger to her temple and began tapping. Those who knew her as well as Grace and Rebecca knew she was cooking up some scheme.

"Why not marry him?" Caroline asked. "I've seen the two of you at church. You are madly in love with each other."

"I suggested as much to Joshua. He was about to propose when the Brannans showed up on his doorstep, so it is not like we were not already headed that direction."

"But?" Rebecca asked.

"He is afraid I will resent him if we rush into marriage to strengthen his case for keeping his daughter. He wants to, as he said, 'lead us' in that direction at the proper time."

"I think that speaks highly of his character," Rebecca said.

Grace's shoulders sagged. She wanted to help him.

"We can pray," Caroline suggested and then she led them in a prayer asking God for wisdom and patience.

"Thank you," Grace said.

The three women talked at length about their lives. When she grew tired, Grace excused herself. Caroline offered to have Thomas give her a ride home, but she did not want to put out her friend. It was not that far.

As she walked past the town square, she noticed Theodore, her father's secretary, speaking with the Brannans. What business would he have with the couple? She frowned and turned away from the town square and headed toward Joshua's office.

When she stepped into the freight office, he smiled at her as he finished helping a customer. Then he motioned her to come back to his private office.

He kissed her on the cheek. "What brings you out? How

are you feeling? You look tired."

She sat in a chair across from his desk. "I am tired. I was on my way home from a visit with Caroline and Rebecca when I spotted Father's secretary speaking with the Brannans."

Joshua frowned. "You suspect your father has something to do with this?"

"Yes. Theodore would have no business with them. If they are who they claim, then he should be a complete stranger."

He rubbed his chin. "I hadn't considered that they might be frauds. I'll speak to Alex to see if we can dig into their background more. Rachel never mentioned her husband's name, much less any extended family, so I suppose the whole thing could be a farce."

"I'm sorry to say, but this is the kind of underhanded thing my father would do to an enemy."

His features softened. "Oh, Grace. I'm so sorry. I know it breaks your heart that he seems so against me."

Joshua came around the desk and pulled her into his arms.

"I do not want to have to choose between the two of you." Her voice cracked as tears streamed down her face. "I will choose you every time. I just don't want to lose my father."

He stroked her hair. "I know."

The weariness in her soul weighed heavy. She sagged against the man she loved with all her heart.

"Let me take you home."

She nodded and took a seat to wait for him to fetch the carriage.

On the way back to her house, he said, "There is a court date. A week from Tuesday. Alex said that Judge Stanton will be presiding."

"Oh, good," she said, relieved that they would get the judge they hoped for.

He dropped her off and left.

Kingsley greeted her as she stepped into the entryway. She heard voices from her father's study.

"Who is here?"

"Just Theodore."

She frowned and headed toward the stairs. A part of her wanted to confront her father about what she suspected he was doing. Her reason won and she chose to retire to her room.

"Please have Mercy bring up a tray for me at supper time. I am feeling quite tired."

"Yes, Miss Grace."

She held her chin high as she went upstairs. Her father started a war. A war against the man she loved. A war she hoped Father would lose.

CHAPTER 31

Tuesday morning, Joshua's pulse quickened, and his stomach clenched as he walked to the courthouse. He barely slept the night before as his mind churned over all his failures as a father. He may lose Victoria because of it.

Grace walked toward him as he neared the large brick building. She wore a light blue dress that made her gray-blue eyes sparkle. She smiled at him. He could not muster up a smile in return.

"Morning," she greeted him and kissed him on the cheek. "You look tired."

He took off his hat and ran his hand through his hair. "Honestly, I'm a wreck."

She took his hand and interlaced her fingers with his. "Trust God, Joshua."

He held back a snort. It was an easy thing to say and terribly difficult to do. He held the door open for Grace.

"Will Victoria be here?" she asked.

"Miss Bethie is bringing her soon."

A knife twisted deep in his heart. Alex said she would need to be there, but he really did not want his failures aired in front of her or for her to be afraid that she might be taken away from the only parent she had ever known. She was too young to remember Rachel or even her birth father.

Grace rubbed his arm with her other hand. "It will be alright."

When Alex approached them, Joshua released her hand and stepped forward. Alex led him to the courtroom where he and Alex sat at a table. The Brannans and an attorney in a very expensive suit sat at the other table. Grace sat in the row of seats behind him.

The bailiff announced that the courtroom should rise when Judge Stanton entered the room. Once he took his seat, he allowed them to sit.

Joshua fidgeted with a button on his jacket until Alex nudged him. He laid his hands flat on his legs under the table willing his nervous energy to subside.

The court clerk read off some information about the case, then the judge started the proceedings. Joshua's mouth felt incredibly dry. He reached for his glass of water and took a swig. A light hand touched his shoulder and he turned to see Victoria sitting behind him. He squeezed her hand and gave her a reassuring smile that he did not feel.

The judge asked Victoria to come forward and sit in the witness chair.

"What is your name?" he smiled and looked at her.

Her eyes were wide, and she looked over to Joshua. He nodded and smiled.

"Victoria Harrison."

"And how old are you?"

"Eleven."

"Can you tell me about your parents?"

"That's my papa," she said pointing to him. "I love him."

Joshua smiled as his heart filled with pride.

Judge Stanton smiled. "What about your mama?"

"After she died, I went to live with Papa and Uncle Dixon."

"How old were you when she died?"

Victoria looked down at the floor. "Three," she whispered.

Judge Stanton encouraged her. "You are doing great, Victoria. Do you remember anything about your mama?"

"No. Only stories that Papa tells me."

"Alright. Thank you. You can have a seat."

Victoria bolted out of the chair and ran to Joshua. She threw her arms around his neck. He hugged her back, his heart twisting. Then he told her to go sit with Miss Grace and Miss Bethie.

The judge then called him to the witness stand. Once Joshua sat down the council for the Brannans, Mr. Randall, requested that the attorneys speak with the judge. He overheard some of what Mr. Randall said.

"My clients are asking for custody of Victoria because they are the blood relatives of the girl. They also have evidence," he said as he handed the judge a piece of paper, "that Mr. Harrison is an unfit father."

Joshua's stomach churned.

The judge allowed Alex to read the paper. Then Alex shook his head. Joshua was not sure if that meant he should not worry.

Once the judge excused the attorneys, he turned his attention to Joshua. "Mr. Harrison, are you Victoria's birth father?"

"No. I adopted her when she was six."

"Yet, her mother died when she was three. Can you help me understand who cared for Victoria between then?"

"I did, your honor. And my friend Dixon."

"Why did you take over her care?"

Joshua's palms sweat as he told the story of how he knew Rachel and came upon her dying. He tried to keep the story as brief as possible and left out many of the horrible details to spare Victoria. When he glanced over at the Brannans, they looked bored. Not grief stricken. Not upset. Just bored.

"With Rachel's dying words, she asked me to care for Victoria as my own. So that's what I did."

"Why did you wait so long to adopt her?"

"Honestly, it never crossed my mind. She was my daughter. Rachel made it clear what her wishes were. I never considered that some sort of paperwork would be needed until my friend, Dixon, urged me to do so."

The judge asked him questions about Dixon and how long they had known each other. He asked what Joshua did for a living.

"I own a freighting operation."

"Do you travel for work?"

"Yes."

"When you travel, who watches after Victoria?"

"My housekeeper, Miss Bethie."

The judge looked down at the paper Mr. Randall had given him. "Do you know a Miss Carmella Ochato?"

Joshua swallowed hard. He glanced at Alex who gave him a barely perceptible nod.

"Yes."

"Who is she?"

Joshua explained that she had been his housekeeper the last few months they lived in Tucson. Alex cautioned him that morning not to say too much.

Then the judge asked him about the worst possible thing. "Did you ever return home from work or a business trip to find Miss Ochato involved with a man in, say a compromising position?" The judge parsed his words when he glanced over at Victoria.

"Yes."

"What did you do?"

"I fired her immediately and stayed home until I made arrangements to move to Prescott."

Joshua's heart pounded. The judge finished asking him questions and then invited Keira Brannan to come forward.

"How do you know Rachel Feagan?" the judge asked.

"She is my sister."

"And when did you learn she was deceased?"

"A few months ago."

The judge frowned and Joshua held his breath. "So, in eight years' time, you did not think it odd that you had no word from your sister?"

Keira Brannan shifted in her seat. "I… uh…"

"When did you learn that she had a daughter?"

Keira looked at the back corner of the room. She glared.

Joshua turned to follow her line of sight as a man stepped out the door. Grace gasped and whispered loud enough for him to hear. "It's my father."

His jaw tightened. The Brannans had to be frauds, paid off by Grace's father.

The bailiff came up and whispered something in the judge's ear.

"I'm sorry. I know you were hoping for a ruling today, but I have an urgent matter that requires my attention. We will adjourn until tomorrow morning at nine o'clock." He banged the gavel and Joshua jumped.

He turned toward Alex. "What is going on?"

"I'm not sure. It's unusual for the judge to leave hastily like that. It seems we'll be back here in the morning."

Joshua could barely stand it. Another night with no answers.

Grace and Victoria came forward. Miss Bethie said she would see them at home. Victoria hugged her arms around his waist.

"You get to keep me, right Papa?"

"I... Don't know yet." He failed to keep the emotion from his voice. The whole thing ate at him. And to think Simon Talbert could really be behind it all. He had not wanted to believe it when Grace brought it up the other day. But catching a glimpse of him leaving the courtroom. He shook his head.

Alex told him that he would let him know if he heard anything and suggested they all go about their day. Like he could think about anything until he heard from the judge's mouth that Victoria was his.

Grace suggested they eat an early dinner at one of the restaurants in town. He followed her. Throughout the meal she did her best to distract Victoria. Joshua barely ate. His stomach hurt and his mind whirled. He could not lose his daughter.

What would happen to her if she went to live with those strangers?

He clenched his jaw tightly to stem the emotion that threatened to drown him.

Grace said her farewells. Joshua did not blame her. He was terrible company. Then he took his daughter home for what he hoped would not be her last night in his home.

CHAPTER 32

"Where is he?" Grace growled when Kingsley opened the door.

"In his office." Kingsley quickly stepped aside as Grace strode straight for her father's office.

"Have you no heart at all?" she accused him as she tapped her foot rapidly on the floor. She crossed her arms as she stood inches from his desk.

"What are you talking about?" he asked.

"I saw you at the courthouse today. Why would you do this to Joshua?"

Her father's face went crimson. "Why would I do this! You did this, Grace, when you refused to break it off with him!"

Her mouth gaped open. She quickly closed it.

"You don't even know him. He is a good man and a good father. His daughter has never known her mother or any extended family. She only knows him. Would you really see her stripped from the only father she has ever known?"

Her father frowned and held her gaze.

"Would you have let someone take me away from you? Can you imagine me at eleven? If Mama had died years earlier and you raised me—"

"You leave your mother out of this." He slammed his

palm down on his desk and stood. "You have no right to speak about her this way."

He rounded the desk and stood inches from her.

She still remembered the slap across her face the last time she crossed him, so she backed down. It was no use anyway. He was determined to destroy Joshua no matter what she said. She could see that as his gray-blue eyes shot daggers through her heart.

That was the moment she realized, she did have to choose between her father and Joshua. Father forced the decision.

A tear slid down her cheek as she backed away. She turned and headed to her room.

"Mercy!" she called out as she climbed stairs. Though she called the maid's name, a part of her hoped her father would show Joshua mercy and end his malicious quest.

When she entered her room, Mercy followed close behind.

"Help me pack a trunk."

"Are you going somewhere, Miss Grace?" The maid wrung her hands.

"Yes. I'm moving out."

Mercy gasped then recovered quickly and started laying out several of Grace's favorite dresses and hats. She folded each garment with care and placed it in the trunk while Grace gathered her Bible and journal and a faded picture of Mama.

She looked around the room trying to decide what else she might wish to take then she decided that she could always send word for Mercy to bring more things later.

When Mercy finished filling the trunk, she asked her to send Kingsley up. Within minutes he was at her door.

"I'm going to Lancaster's Boardinghouse. Please arrange

for my trunk to be delivered shortly."

He nodded and she walked out of her room and down the stairs.

Her father stood blocking the doorway.

"Step aside," she demanded.

"Grace, what are you doing?"

"I'm leaving."

He frowned and crossed his arms over his chest. "You are not."

"Yes, I am. I can decide for myself where I want to live and who I want to live my life with. You have gone out of your way to make it clear that you do not approve of my choices."

Her hands shook.

"You cannot marry him."

"You have lost the right to have a say." She lifted her chin and tried to look braver than she felt.

Father scowled for another minute, then he moved out of her way.

She opened the door as she heard Kingsley grunting under the weight of carrying her trunk down the stairs. Then she walked out the door without looking back.

Once she was out of sight of her home, she stopped and took a deep breath. She finally stood up to her father and it felt horrible. Her stomach twisted. Her legs shook. Her heart ached.

He had left her no choice.

She walked to Lancaster's hoping they had a room available. Though her decision had been hasty, she did not regret it.

A few minutes later she arrived at Lancaster's Boardinghouse. Annabel greeted her as she entered the parlor.

"Miss Talbert. Have you come to visit with Mama?"

Grace smiled. "I've come to see about a room first."

"Oh. Let me get Mama."

Grace paced in front of the fireplace.

"Grace," Millie's soft voice came from behind her. "Annabel tells me you want to rent a room?"

"Yes," her voice cracked at the sight of a friendly face.

"Come sit for a moment. Tell me what happened."

Grace sat in a chair next to Millie and shared everything that happened. How her father was determined to hurt Joshua. How she stood up to him. How she now had no place to live.

"Not to worry," Millie said as she squeezed her hand. "We have a room available in the new building that I think you will like. Would you like to see it?"

"Yes."

Millie stood and walked Grace over to the newly constructed second house on the property.

"We take all our meals in my home, so there is no dining room and only a small kitchen. I have both a first floor room and a second floor room available, though I think the one on the second floor is furnished more like what you are accustomed to."

Millie showed her both rooms and Grace agreed that she liked the second floor room better. The sitting room had a sweeping view of the town square. The bedroom was almost as large as her bedroom had been. There were double doors to separate the two spaces if she desired to close off the bedroom and entertain a guest or two in the sitting room.

"Of course, the parlor downstairs is open to all our guests," Millie said.

The room also had a private washroom with running water.

"It's perfect," Grace said. She counted out the payment

for the first month and handed it to Millie. "Kingsley is sending over a trunk. I may have more things coming in a few days."

"I will have Paul bring up your trunk when it arrives."

"Thank you."

Millie paused as she opened the door. "I'm so sorry, Grace. I will be praying for you. I do hope your father will come around."

She gave Grace a hug and left.

Grace sighed as she looked around the room. Somehow independence did not feel as good as she hoped. She always assumed she would leave her father's home to go to her husband's home. Until that day she never considered living on her own.

She looked out the window and noticed the sun setting. It was too late to see Joshua tonight. She would tell him in the morning.

A half hour later, Paul Lancaster knocked on the door. She opened it and he set the trunk in her bedroom.

"We hope you enjoy the space," he said before he left.

Grace opened the trunk and unpacked her things. There was a small wardrobe and dresser in the bedroom. She hung her dresses in the wardrobe and placed her hats on the shelf above the dresses. Then she set two pairs of shoes beside the wardrobe. Her unmentionables and nightgowns took up the better portion of the dresser drawers. Perhaps she would make do with what she brought.

She took her Bible, journal, and picture of Mama into the sitting room. Then she sat in one of the pink upholstered chairs and stared out the window.

Placing a hand over her gunshot wound, she sighed. Though it had healed and no longer pained her, she did wonder if there was any lasting damage. She was so busy the last few days supporting Joshua that she did not think about it. The doctor told her his concerns about her ability to have children, something she did not want to burden Joshua with while things were so uncertain with his daughter.

A tear slid down her cheek. She wanted children of her own. How ironic that in her attempt to save that little Indian boy she may have destroyed her chance to have children.

She dreamed of a house full of children, with Joshua by her side. Some children lost their family, like Victoria. Others would be theirs. The idea took root. Perhaps they could start an orphanage, a place where children could receive love. A home where they could thrive. A place to belong.

If she and Joshua created such a place, she could easily give up her position with the Women's Aid Society. Someone else would step up to the challenge and manage the organization while she poured her whole heart into making a home for children in need.

Grace yawned as the stress of the day took its toll. She readied herself for bed and turned down the lamp. She would think on the idea more. When the time was right, she would share the dream with Joshua.

CHAPTER 33

The next morning, Joshua saw Grace leaving Lancaster's boardinghouse. He frowned. What was she doing there?

Victoria waved and called out, "Miss Grace!"

Grace caught up to them. "Morning," she said breathlessly.

"Victoria, can you walk on ahead?" he asked. She bound-ed off.

Grace took his hand and he stiffened as they walked.

"There's been a development with my father," she said.

He stopped and turned toward her. His anger faded when he saw the glistening of her eyes. "What happened?"

She sniffed. "He is behind everything. He did not come right out and say it, but he paid off the Brannans to file this case to hurt you."

Joshua's jaw tightened and his arm twitched. How dare her father come after his daughter.

"He insisted again that I break things off with you, so I moved out."

"Did he throw you out?" So, help him if that man laid a finger on her.

"No, it was my choice." She dabbed at a tear in the corner of her eye. "I'm so sorry. I know you have enough on your mind as it is. But I thought you would want to know."

He took a deep breath and let it out slowly. He took her

face in his hands and searched her eyes. "I do want to know even if the timing is difficult. Did he hurt you?"

"No. Other than a broken heart," her voice caught. "I'll be fine."

He kissed her forehead and wrapped her in his arms. "I'm so sorry he made you choose."

"Me too." Her voice was muffled against his chest. She lifted her head. "I choose you, Joshua. Every time, I will choose you."

His eyes burned. Her words filled up a broken and empty space in his heart. His beautiful Grace chose him. He knew it already, yet hearing the words made him want to shout from the town square. He was loved by the woman he loved more than life.

Joshua convinced his heart to settle down. "We should go so we aren't late."

She nodded and held onto the crook of his arm as they walked the rest of the way to the courthouse. When they arrived, Alex paced outside.

"There you are," he said. "The judge wants to see us in his chambers."

Joshua stepped forward with Grace still holding onto his arm and Victoria holding his other hand.

"Ah, just attorneys, Joshua, and the Brannans," Alex clarified.

Joshua hugged Victoria and asked her to wait there with Grace.

"Go," Grace said. "I'll be praying."

Alex led Joshua into the courthouse and down a side hall. He stopped in front of a room with Judge Stanton's name on it. He knocked and the judge told them to come in.

"Take a seat. The Brannans should be here shortly."

A half hour later the Brannans' attorney arrived without them. Joshua's heart lodged in his throat. He fidgeted with lint on his pants. He paced the tiny room until the judge gave him a warning look. Then he sat down.

Another hour later and the bailiff entered the room. "They skipped town."

Joshua's head snapped up and he met the judge's gaze.

"Hmm. As I suspected," Judge Stanton said. He turned his attention to Mr. Randall. "Do you know where your clients are going?"

"No, your honor. When I last spoke to them, they indicated they would be here today."

"Very well," Judge Stanton said. "We'll proceed without them."

Joshua's stomach flipped. If he had eaten breakfast, he was certain he would have lost it by then.

"It has come to my attention that the Brannans could provide no proof of their claim. Furthermore, there have been allegations brought before the court that they knowingly submitted a fraudulent claim. This information, along with the fact that they skipped town, leads me to believe the allegations are true. Therefore, I am throwing this case out."

Joshua's eyes could not focus on anything in the room. He felt dizzy.

"Mr. Harrison, I am sorry that you have been dragged through such a horrible ordeal. I hope you will accept the court's gratitude for your cooperation. In the end justice succeeded."

Joshua cleared his throat. "Is Victoria… Does she…"

"Yes, Mr. Harrison, Victoria remains your legal charge."

He coughed as the air felt like it was sucked out of the room. He managed to regain control after a few seconds.

"Thank you, your honor."

The judge dismissed them. Joshua ran down the hall and out the front doors until he saw his daughter. Then he gathered her in his arms and hugged her tightly.

"Papa, you're hurting me."

"I'm sorry, Pumpkin," he said as tears streamed down his face. He loosened his grip some.

"What happened?" Grace asked as she placed a hand on his shoulder.

"The judge dropped the case," Alex said as he joined them. "Turns out it was a fraudulent claim. The Brannans skipped town this morning."

Victoria squealed and hugged him close. Grace kneeled and hugged them both.

Joshua's heart nearly burst. His family was safe. It was his job to make sure Grace became a permanent part of his family soon.

He released his hold on his girls and stood. His stomach growled.

"Let's go get some breakfast."

They agreed and he took each of their hands and led them to the café. They ordered and he smiled at them both.

When he caught Grace staring out the window, his joy dimmed. She sacrificed her relationship with her father to be with them. He would honor that sacrifice.

———

Grace noticed Joshua watching her, so she smiled. She took his hand and squeezed it. "I'm so glad everything turned out fine."

"Not everything," he said.

Her smile faded and she nodded slowly, knowing he referred to her fractured relationship with her father. It hurt, but she did not want to dwell on it.

After they finished breakfast, she walked home with Joshua and Victoria. He let Miss Bethie know the outcome of the case before he joined her in the parlor. Victoria played outside while Miss Bethie washed their laundry.

They sat in two chairs facing the fireplace. The same place he had been going to propose.

"So much has happened in the last few weeks," she began. "We haven't been able to talk about…"

Her heart tightened.

Joshua took her hand and smiled.

"I might not be able to have children," she blurted out. "The doctor thinks the gunshot wound may have—"

"I know. He mentioned it to me before he realized we were not married."

Her breath left her lungs in a whoosh. "And you still want me?"

He moved to kneel on the floor in front of her. "Yes. Of course, I do. Whether we have children of our own or not, I want you, Grace Talbert. That's what I was trying to say the other day before we were interrupted. I want you to be my wife, to be Victoria's mother. You are the only woman I have ever truly loved, and you love me back."

Grace smiled through her tears. "Yes, I want you too, Joshua. And Victoria."

He stood and pulled her to him. Then he lowered his lips to hers and kissed her deeply until she moaned. Then he released her.

Though he left her breathless, she still needed to say more. "Please, sit," she said.

"I was thinking and praying about what I would do if I married you. I mean when I marry you. I would like to build an orphanage, Joshua. I want a house full of children who need our love. Children like Victoria who lost her parents. Children like that poor starving Indian boy. Children who need a home and parents who will love them unconditionally."

Joshua slowly nodded.

"I would step down from the Women's Aid Society. No more risky trips to Camp Date Creek. Instead, my focus would be on our family whether we have our own children or not."

Slowly his lips stretched into a smile. "That is a vision I can fully embrace, Grace. Oddly, until you just said this, I hadn't realized how both you and I care so deeply for orphaned and hurting children. I think your idea is worth our effort and the cost. I would love to love the unloved children that come into our home with you."

"Do you think Victoria will mind?" she asked scared that she might not want siblings.

Joshua laughed. "I think Victoria will love it as much as I do."

Grace let out a long breath. They sat together in silence for some time before he offered to walk her back to the boardinghouse to her temporary home. She hoped he would officially propose soon so she could start her life with him.

CHAPTER 34

Joshua's timing might not be the best, he thought as he examined the property Alex Glassman mentioned to him. Grace was busy finalizing plans for the harvest festival in a few days.

He did not want to wait much longer to propose. The sooner he proposed, the sooner they could marry, and the sooner they could build their dreams together.

He walked the length of the property, surprised to find such a large lot available in town. It was really two adjacent lots. When he told Alex about their plans for an orphanage, he suggested the property and convinced Joshua that the town would approve an orphanage in the space. He would do the paperwork whenever Joshua and Grace were ready.

Smiling, Joshua thought how odd it was that he had become friends with Alex Glassman, Grace's former suitor. Alex helped him so much with the custody case. A few days after it was all over, Alex stopped by to see how they were getting along. Honestly, Joshua thought his new friend might be a bit lonely and longing for a family of his own, despite his final days of his campaign for District Attorney.

The lot was surrounded by one long white picket fence. There were a few charred boards where a building once stood. Alex said it had burned down several years ago. The grass on the lot looked healthy, though a little overgrown.

Two large cottonwood trees stood guard along the back end of the property.

He closed his eyes, and he could visualize the house he wanted to build. Three stories. A long sweeping porch with two porch swings, one on each side. A large parlor where they would gather daily. At Christmas time, they would decorate it with boughs of pine and a large tree. A bedroom with a private washroom for him and Grace.

Heat warmed his face as he thought about how special that room would be. A retreat away from the noise of the rest of the house.

He opened his eyes. They would need a large dining room table if they were going to adopt a dozen or so children. At least four more bedrooms on the second floor with one or two more washrooms. The third floor would be for staff.

He could already hear the home filling with laughter.

Joshua made his way back to Alex's office to finalize the purchase of the property. With deed in hand, he ordered a picnic meal from one of the restaurants, complete with fancy sandwiches of course. Then he checked his watch. Time to pick up Grace.

He tucked the deed into his shirt pocket. Then he headed over to Lancaster's. Grace was waiting for him in one of the rockers on the front porch. Maybe he would make them a few rocking chairs for their home too.

"Good evening, Miss Talbert. Would you care to join me for a picnic?"

He winked at her, and she blushed.

"I would love to Mr. Harrison."

She placed her hand in the crook of his arm. As they walked through town, he caught her looking around.

"Where are we going?" she asked.

"It's a surprise." He hoped it would be the best surprise of her life.

————

Grace did not recognize the part of town where Joshua was leading her. They missed the turn for his house. They went past a park and climbed up a rather steep hill. Then at the top, he stopped in front of an empty lot.

She quirked an eyebrow as he opened the gate on a white picket fence.

"Will the owners mind if we picnic on their property?" she asked.

He grinned. "No, they will not."

She followed him still very confused about what they were doing there. He shook out a blanket and set it on the ground. Then he set down the basket.

"What is this place?" she asked, her curiosity getting the best of her.

"Let me lead, Grace," he said as he placed his hand on the small of her back. "Trust me, it is worth the wait."

She sighed.

Then he got down on one knee in front of her. Oh! It was happening.

"Grace, you know I love you, but I'll tell you again. I loved you from the first moment I saw you. You captured my heart in the grasslands and you've carefully tended to it ever since. You are the one I have waited so long for. So, I will ask you at last—"

"Yes!"

He laughed. "I'm not done yet."

"Oh, continue," she giggled.

"Will you be my wife?"

"Yes!"

He stood and pulled her into his arms. He kissed her with a new level of passion that left her feeling a little light-headed when he pulled away.

"Now that we've had dessert," he teased, "how about some supper before it gets too dark to see. I forgot the candles."

She laughed and took a seat beside him on the blanket.

"Your fancy sandwich my dear."

"Is it chicken or ham?"

"Chicken. I believe that's your favorite."

"Mmm. I would eat any fancy sandwich you give me."

"Oh, good, you take the ham this time." He swapped sandwiches with her.

She took a bite and looked around the property. "What is this place?"

"This, right here?" He wiggled his eyebrows. "This is where our bedroom will be."

Her breath caught and heat warmed her face. She stood and ran a few feet away, hoping to still her pulse. "And this?"

"That's the parlor. We need a large parlor if we're going to adopt a dozen children." He laughed as he caught up to her.

She sidestepped him. "A dozen you say? Why not a baker's dozen or two dozen?"

Grace moved toward the back yard a few more feet. "And this?"

"The place we'll have dessert."

"I thought you said our bedroom was over there."

He caught her in his arms. "No, this is the dining room. The place we will have actual desserts, like cake, pudding, whatever you want."

"Mmm. Sounds nice."

She wiggled free of his embrace and move back a few more feet. "And this?"

"The kitchen. Don't worry, I won't ask you to make more than eggs."

She giggled enjoying his teasing. "What if I want to learn how to make more than eggs? Would you teach me how to make that delicious pot roast?"

Joshua captured her again. "I don't know. It's a Harrison family recipe."

"But, I'll be a Harrison."

"Oh fine. I'll show you in a few weeks then."

Her laughter faded. "A few weeks."

"How do you feel about a quick wedding?" he asked as he trailed kisses down her neck.

"Mmm. I might consider it."

Then he kissed her ear lobe.

"More convincing," she whispered.

Then he kissed her hard on the lips searching and probing. Fire spread through her body to the tips of her fingers as she kissed him back. His hands pressed her closer until she thought she might not be able to stand it any longer. She eased away.

"Alright," Grace said. "Two weeks from now. That is my final offer."

"Sold."

He led her back to their half-eaten meal.

"Joshua, I love the place, but I think it might be a little drafty to move into after the wedding."

He chuckled. "We can live at my place until we build the house. Oh, and in case you were going to ask, yes, there will be plenty of rooms for our children."

CHAPTER 35

Grace woke after a restless night. It was her wedding day. It should be the happiest day of her life. It almost was. Almost except her father still would not speak to her.

How hard it was going to be to walk down the aisle later that day without him. She told Joshua if her father still refused to see her or be a part of her life, she would walk the aisle alone. He had been so supportive and agreed that she could do whatever she wanted.

Mama would have liked Joshua. She imagined several times throughout her sleepless night telling Mama all about him. Mama would have liked his laugh. She would have liked the way he loved Grace so completely. Most of all, Mama would be very happy she chose a love match.

She sighed as she readied herself for her wedding. She was both nervous and excited at the same time. She was a little nervous about her wedding night, not really sure what to expect. Until she reminded herself that women had been marrying since the beginning of time. She figured she had nothing to worry about. She knew her husband would calm her fears.

Husband.

Grace let out a shaky breath. Joshua would be hers today. She would be his.

She thought back to the day she broke off her courtship

with Alex Glassman, an odd thing to think of on her wedding day. Yet, she never once regretted that decision. It made the way for her to explore a relationship with spark and passion with Joshua.

A knock sounded on the door.

"Miss Grace," Mercy said. "I'm here to help."

She opened the door of the pastor's office where she would get ready. Mercy entered with her.

"Mr. Harrison came by the house last week. He told us about your wedding. Your father allowed us to have the day off."

Grace held her breath. "Is Daddy coming?"

Mercy shook her head. "Mr. Harrison tried very hard to convince him to come and to let the animosity between them go, but Mr. Talbert would not budge."

Grace's heart ached and leaped all at the same time. Joshua tried to get Daddy to reconcile. What a wonderful gift, even though Daddy remained too stubborn to change.

Mercy helped Grace into her wedding dress. The dressmaker worked a miracle to get it ready on such short notice. It helped that Grace had a white dress to start from. Mercy fashioned her hair with ringlets trailing down her back. She pulled the sides of her hair back with two ivory combs, the ones Mama gave her. Then Mercy pinned her veil in place.

"You look stunning," Mercy announced. "Mr. Harrison will be very pleased."

"Thank you, Mercy. Will Esther and Kingsley be at the wedding?"

"Yes, Miss Grace. Shall I walk with you to make sure your dress does not get dirty?"

"That would be nice, thank you."

They walked from the church office where she had gotten ready around to the back entrance when the music started.

Mercy and Kingsley held the doors open and Grace stepped into the church. She glanced over her shoulder, still hoping Daddy would come. He did not.

She sighed and took a step forward. Her gaze connected with Joshua's as soon as he was in view. The sheen in his eyes suggested that he might not be as composed as she was. She smiled at him, and he smiled back.

Then she slowly walked down the aisle toward her future and her husband. They said their vows and he was finally hers.

When the pastor told him he could kiss his bride, Joshua dipped her back and kissed her with some restraint. When he finished, he whispered in her ear, "Mrs. Harrison, don't confuse that for dessert. It was more like a tiny petit four."

Grace giggled and followed him out of the church and to the reception in the church yard. Victoria gave her a big hug when they took their seats.

After an hour, Joshua leaned over and whispered to her. "How long do we have to stay?"

Her heart raced at the look of desire in his eyes.

"So, you're ready for dessert, then?" she teased him.

He groaned. "And then some."

They said their farewells to their guests, and he drove her in a carriage to his house. He already arranged for Victoria to stay with Miss Bethie at the ranch for a few days so he could enjoy spoiling his wife for the first few days of their marriage.

When they arrived home, Joshua lifted her in his arms and carried her over the threshold. He kicked the door shut with his foot and took her straight to the bedroom and lavished her with a love she longed for.

EPILOGUE

Prescott, Arizona Territory
November 16, 1877

Joshua's heart sped up as the wagon crested the last hill outside of Prescott. The town filled the valley below. He was almost home. He was not due back for a few more days, but he left early hoping to make it back that day, his fifth anniversary with Grace.

The trip to California would hopefully be his last trip away. He originally planned to send Dixon until he learned that Dixon's wife, Sophie, was due any day now.

"Joshua," little Allan got his attention. "Is this my home now?"

His heart twisted. When he found six-year-old Allan on the streets of San Francisco begging for food, he brought him with him. No six-year-old should have to beg for food.

"Yes."

"What is the orphanage like?" he asked for the hundredth time.

"Grace, you can call her Mama Grace if you like, has a heart bigger than the ocean. She and I will love you as our own. You'll get three meals a day, a bed of your own, and you'll have five other brothers to play with."

"Five?"

"And then there are six girls, well seven if you include my daughter Victoria, though she is almost grown."

Joshua pulled the wagon to a stop behind the freight office. Ira came out to unload the few things he brought back for the business. The primary purpose of the trip had been to hire a manager to take over his late father's freighting business and consolidate it with Joshua's business. He also had the opportunity to spend a few days with his brother and his wife who cared for his aging mother. He wished he could convince Mama to move to Prescott, but she had no desire to leave the bay area.

When the freight was unloaded, Ira volunteered to drive them to the house and take the wagon and horses back to the freight stables.

Home. They moved in four years ago, the process taking longer than he expected. It was a large home with a sweeping front porch. Three stories tall. The first floor included a parlor, library, large kitchen, dining room, laundry room, and his and Grace's bedroom. The second floor held six bedrooms. The third floor attic was one large room with several beds for the staff. That house fulfilled Grace's dream to start an orphanage, a dream he accepted and made his own.

He helped Allan down from the wagon and set their luggage and two crates on the porch.

"Are you ready? It will be noisy."

"Yes, Joshua."

He hoped when the boy grew more comfortable with him, that he would call him Papa or Papa Josh as many of the children did. As he opened the front door, laughter greeted him.

"Go, Martin! You almost got him this time," Grace encouraged.

"Henry, almost there!" Victoria exclaimed.

He held Allan's hand and led him into the parlor where all the ruckus was. Martin and Henry were both ten years old. They were blindfolded on the floor playing a game of cudgel. Their left hands grasped each other. In their right hand, they each held a rolled-up newspaper. The two took turns swatting at each other. Finally, Martin hit Henry, winning the game.

Joshua laughed deeply. He so enjoyed watching the boys expend some energy with the game.

"Papa Josh!" The girls squealed in unison.

Before he knew it, he and Allan were swallowed up by Alice, Cora, Mabel, Wilma, Pearl, and Beulah. Victoria, at seventeen, hung back knowing she would have his full attention later. A few more seconds went by, and the boys gathered around too. There was Henry and Martin. Then Hugh, Noah, and Loren.

"Who's this?" observant Loren asked.

"This is Allan. He is your new brother."

Joshua's heart warmed as all the children quickly welcomed the young boy.

He searched the room for Grace and left the children to greet his wife. She looked particularly luminous today. Her eyes lit when he stood in front of her.

Then he took her in his arms and kissed her. Not like what he wanted to, but what was appropriate with such a large audience. The boys made fake choking and barfing sounds. He did not care. It was good for them to see how a man treats his wife.

"Happy anniversary," he said.

Grace's smile lit the room. "I can't believe you made it back in time. I was not expecting you yet."

"I hope you have room in your heart for number thirteen. Allan needs a home."

She giggled. "I hope you have room in your heart for number fourteen in say five months."

Joshua's heart leaped to his throat. "Are you?"

"Yes." The word left her lips on a breath.

They both thought she might not be able to have children. The bullet wound she incurred at Camp Date Creek over five years ago left them wondering. Oh, what wonderful news!

He hugged her even closer. Then he suddenly released her. "I didn't hurt you, did I?"

She laughed. "I'm not a porcelain doll, Joshua. I'm just pregnant."

"A baby. We've never had a baby before. Wasn't Pearl the youngest when she came to live with us at two?"

Grace nodded.

Esther rang a loud cowbell signaling it was time for supper. She and Mercy came to work for them when Simon Talbert passed three years ago. Kingsley returned to London. Grace's heart ached over the broken relationship and Joshua was disappointed that her father never accepted him or showed interest in their large family, other than keeping Grace as his sole heir.

"You can sit by me, Allan," Martin said.

The children made their way to the sink to wash up, supervised by Victoria.

Joshua took advantage of the empty parlor and kissed his wife deeply, leaving her a little unstable when they joined the children in the dining room.

"You always did like your dessert before supper," Grace teased under her breath.

He took his place at the head of the table. Grace sat to his right. Victoria sat at the foot of the table to help keep supper a civilized affair. He looked at each child, his heart so full.

Who could have predicted when he spotted Grace at her mother's funeral, that they would become husband and wife, much less have a full house. Both he and Grace had found such deep joy out of their mourning over lost loved ones.

"Papa," Victoria prompted him. "Will you say grace?"

He made eye contact with each child. "I just want you to know how much I love each and every one of you." Then he turned to Grace and whispered, "You most of all."

AUTHOR'S NOTE

A long time ago, 2010 to be precise, I first developed and introduced Joshua Harrison as a character. When he failed to win Hannah's heart in *A Dream Unfolding*, my first novel, the idea for this story started to develop. Unfortunately, Joshua's story did not fit with the theme of Prescott Pioneers, so I set my ideas aside and focused on other stories.

When I created Grace Talbert's character in *Hidden Prospects*, I knew I eventually wanted her to be a leading lady and have her own story. I always pictured her with a much older man.

As I started to plan the *Desert Manna* series, a match between Joshua and Grace was destined. I had written Joshua's rich back story of unrequited love with Rachel Feagan years ago. The idea to make Joshua a never-have-been-married single dad came to me 2021. I'm so glad his character developed in the way that he did.

In so many romance novels, it seems like the topic of unrequited love is rarely told. I understand why. The reader wants a happy ending with two people who love each other. But in real life, unrequited love is so painful. It shapes the way we interact with people we date or even end up marrying. This was a big motivating factor for me in developing Joshua's character. I wanted to display what happens in a man's heart when he feels rejected not just once, but multiple times. No matter how confident a person appears on the outside, the deep wounds of rejection create self-doubt and insecurity. This is Joshua's story.

In an early version of *Beauty for Ashes* (book 1), I had written some Tolkepaya characters as an antagonist for Perry Quinn. I did a lot of research about the Yavapai and their subtribe called Tolkepaya. The stories in *Joy for Mourning* about the "Yuman-Apache" came out of that research. The Tolkepaya were called "Apache" or "Yuman-Apache" by the whites even though they were a distinctly different group of people from the Apache. The battle scene in *Joy for Mourning* came out of that research. The dates may not be exact, but sometime in September of 1872, the Tolkepaya and Yavapai attacked General Crook and his men at Camp Date Creek. They were not successful in their uprising and showed up to the reservation days later seeking asylum from Crook. They were granted it.

Perhaps one day I will write the story of the Tolkepaya characters. But for now, know that I carefully researched what really happened from both their perspective and the perspective of the whites. It was so much fun to write Grace as an unconventional champion for their cause. There were many real whites in history who were advocates for the native tribes of Arizona.

You might question my decision to include Joshua's torture by the Indians. This was based on a firsthand account from some Irish settlers who settled in the Gila River Basin. They were tormented by the real Apache. A woman who was widowed recounted her story of how the Indians left dead animals on her doorstep or body parts of dead people. That's where the inspiration for Joshua's torture and Rachel's death came from.

In the history of Arizona, great atrocities were committed by whites, Indians, and Mexicans. No one is innocent and no one is all evil either. Each people group had their motivations and justifications for the actions they took.

Anyway, I tried to handle this difficult topic in a fair way through the characters of Grace and Joshua.

I hope that you enjoyed reading their story.

Karen Baney

Want More Arizona Territory Romance?

Get a FREE novella featuring characters connected to the Colter Sons series! Plus exclusive updates on new releases, special offers, and historical insights from the frontier.

Subscribe at: books.karenbaney.com/larson-christmas

ABOUT THE AUTHOR

Karen Baney is passionate about writing stories full of flawed characters. She enjoys weaving together stories of second chances, redemption, and overcoming personal trials. As a transplant to Arizona, she loves researching the state's history and finding ways to seamlessly incorporate real history and real settings into her novels. In addition to writing and speaking, Karen works as a Software Development Manager for a Christian ministry.

Her faith plays an important role both in her life and in her writing. Karen and her husband, Jim, make their home in Gilbert, Arizona, with their two dogs, Bella and Daisy. Both Jim and Karen are active at Rock Point Church in Queen Creek, Arizona.

Discover faith-laced stories with characters who feel like lifelong friends.

Visit www.karenbaney.com to discover more historical romance series set in the American West. Follow Karen's writing journey and get behind-the-scenes glimpses of her research adventures on social media.

Facebook:	@AuthorKarenBaney
X:	@karen_baney
Instagram:	@AuthorKarenBaney
BookBub:	Follow Karen Baney for new release alerts

BOOKS BY KAREN BANEY

Historical Western Romance

Prescott Pioneers Series:

Step back in time to the wild, untamed Arizona Territory where survival depends on grit, faith, and the courage to start over. Follow three pioneer families—the Andersons, Colters, and Larsons—as they risk everything for the promise of a new life in a land that demands both strength and hope.

A Dream Unfolding
A Heart Renewed
A Life Restored
A Hope Revealed
Hidden Prospects

Desert Manna Series:

Sometimes the most beautiful love stories bloom in the desert. Set in the growing frontier town of Prescott during the early 1870s, these tender romances follow women rebuilding their lives after heartbreak and the unexpected men who help them discover that second chances at love are worth the risk. Set in Prescott, Arizona between 1871 - 1873.

Beauty for Ashes
Joy for Mourning
Oaks of Justice

Colter Sons Series:

Power, legacy, and forbidden love collide in this sweeping family saga set in the Arizona Territory. The Colter ranch empire has weathered decades of frontier life, but now family secrets and buried betrayals threaten to destroy everything. As five brothers—and one resilient sister—navigate the treacherous waters of love, loss, and redemption, they must decide what's worth fighting for. Set in Prescott and other locations within the Arizona Territory in 1887 - 1906.

The Reluctant Cattleman
The Roaming Adventurer
The Railroad Magnate
The Resourceful Stockman
The Restless Wrangler
The Resilient Bride

Larson Sisters Series
Meet the next generation! These delightful novellas follow the three daughters of Adam and Julia Larson from the *Prescott Pioneers Series* as they navigate love, courtship, and finding their own happily ever afters in territorial Arizona in 1886 – 1894.

In Love at Christmas
In Love with the Rancher
In Love with the Horse Trainer

Contemporary Romance

Vargas Ranch Series:
Love is in the air at the Vargas Guest Ranch & Resort near Wickenburg, Arizona. Meet the Vargas family—five swoon-worthy brothers and their cousins who live by their family motto: "We do not deviate from the Lord's plan."

These rugged cowboys run a successful working ranch and luxury resort while navigating the rollercoaster of finding true love.

Falling for a Fake Cowboy
Falling for a Real Cowboy
Honeymoon with a Real Cowboy
Falling for a Shy Cowboy
Falling for a Bossy Cowboy
Falling for a Smart Cowboy
Falling for a Humbug Cowboy
Falling for a Devoted Cowgirl
Falling for a Pregnant Cowgirl
Falling for a Cowboy's Legacy

Steadfast Love Series:

The *Steadfast Love* series follows a close-knit group of friends as they navigate the beautiful mess of modern life in the Phoenix area—workplace drama, complicated families, and love that shows up when they least expect it. These contemporary romances blend emotional depth with authentic faith, reminding us that even when life unravels, God's love never does.

The Heart I Rescue (prequel)
The Air I Breathe

Her life hangs by a thread. His heart is closed off.

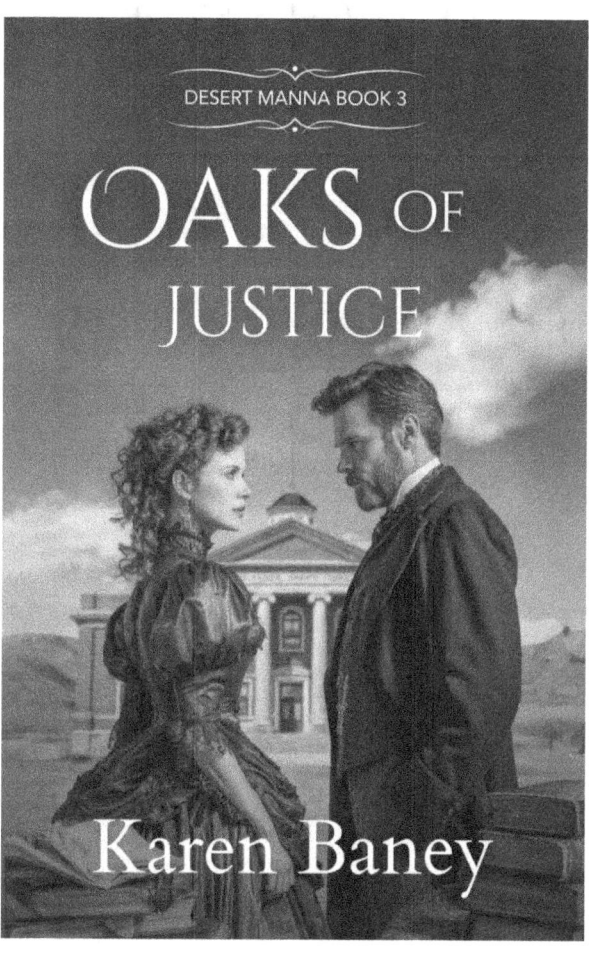

In the courtroom, the stakes are high but love may be the fiercest battle of all.

Mel Larson is one of the few female attorneys in the Arizona Territory, fighting for justice in a world that rarely welcomes her. When threats force her to flee to Prescott, she takes on a murder case that pits her against Alex Glassman— the town's relentless new District Attorney.

Alex has sworn off love after heartbreak. But Mel's fire and conviction shake his resolve, even as the case twists toward danger. When her life is on the line, Alex must choose between duty and the woman who's captured his heart.

Set in the rugged 1870s frontier, this Christian historical romance is a powerful story of justice, redemption, and the love that rises when everything else falls away.

DESERT LIFE MEDIA

———

Desert Life Media: *There Is Life in The Desert*

Entertainment-first Christian fiction set in the Southwest, featuring redemption, family, and faith

Publishing clean, wholesome, and uplifting fiction since 2010

———

desertlifemedia.com

www.ingramcontent.com/pod-product-compliance
Lightning Source LLC
Chambersburg PA
CBHW051947220626
47052CB00004B/827